ME AND MISTER CHIPS

a boy's adventures with his puppy

Louis W. Hirschmann

ISBN-13: 9798327499355
ISBN-10: 1477123456

Cover design by: Jimmy & Mr. Chips
Library of Congress Control Number: 2018675309
Printed in the United States of America

CONTENTS

ME AND MISTER CHIPS

A BOY'S ADVENTURES WITH HIS PUPPY

BOOK I: GOODBYE SCHOPENHAUER

CHAPTER ONE:
A KNOCK ON
THE HEAD

Spring 1958

I t was early June and grammar school was out for the year! Waking up to bright sunshine pouring through my opened curtains on that first Saturday of freedom from classes, I looked over at my miniature German Schnauzer Mr. Chips, who was sitting upright on the built-in toy chest by my bedroom windowsill.

Mr. Chips had a quizzical expression as he looked out the window at Elm Ridge Drive and then back at me in bed, as if to say, "what are we going to do today?"

"It's vacation time, so how about an adventure, Mr. Chips?" I asked him, "just you and I!"

Mr. Chips wagged his tail, as if to say 'yes'! And with that, Schopenhauer, my golden retriever puppy, yawned, stretched and shook himself in the streaming rays of sunshine, his hairs floating this way and that all about our bedroom. Then, he came over to my lower bunk bed to nuzzle me.

"Shhhh, Schopenhauer! You don't wan'na wake up Alec in the upper bunk!" I whispered to the golden, as Mr. Chips let out a loud bark of annoyance because he was being briefly left out of the conversation.

"Shhhhhh, you guys!" we heard from the top bunk, as my older brother Alec rolled over and fell back to sleep.

"Everyone be still!" I admonished my puppies, "don't disturb the doctor!" I laughed because I knew that Alec would be an MD someday like our deceased father, grandfather and stepfather.

"It's all right, Mr. Chips, we won't make any plans without consulting you!" I giggled quietly as I got out of bed, went into the bathroom and, foosh, brushed my teeth, gargled, then threw on a pair of jeans and a short sleeve shirt.

With Mr. Chips and Schopenhauer dutifully following me, I went downstairs and greeted Mother, who was already having her coffee and discussing the evening dinner plans with our big black Jamaican maid, Lo.

"Hello, Jeffrey dear!" Mother said, "and Lo,"

she added, not skipping a beat, "that'll be steak for seven at 6:30 pm, including you two and served medium, ordered from the butcher along with baked potato and green beans to be delivered from the grocer in Hubbard Woods, along with salad, fresh fruit and the usual relishes from Anton's in Northbrook, French rolls from one of the delis in Glencoe and wine from our cellar, dear, thank you," Mother stated summarily, after which Lo quietly departed.

Mother ran a tight ship, that was for sure; and Lo knew just what to do to efficiently acquire and prepare the ingredients for Mother's requested dinner.

Adolph always said that Mother was the perfect housekeeper because 'she always kept the house'; and I innately understood the clever humor of my stepfather's acknowledgment that, when it came to her homes, she always maintained title to them, while still having generously set up trusts for us kids upon receiving her own inheritance, a remarkably prescient kindness that likely would enhance our adult lives far into the future, a rarity for a young woman in her thirties in the era of the 1950's who wasn't vastly wealthy despite her extraordinary thoughtfulness.

"Your mother is one in a million," our stepfather Adolph said; and of course, she was!

Poking her head back into the dining room,

Lo said, "I'll git Massa Jeff's rice crispies and glass o' o j, ma'am!" Then, she scurried off back into the kitchen after she'd written down Mother's wish list for the evening meal.

"I have the ladies coming over for luncheon and canasta later this morning, dear," Mother said, "so please make yourself scarce and go off and entertain yourself. Your older brother and sister have got some plan or another with the Skolsky kids and your stepfather Adolph has already left to make his early rounds at Wyler Memorial Hospital in town," she added.

"I'm going to take Mr. Chips and Schopenhauer for a walk and a little adventure over past Skokie Ridge near Hohlfelder Road!" I announced confidently, having no idea what I was going to do other than enjoy my first late spring day of freedom from the drudgery of the school year. And yes, summer, a limitless horizon of fun and free time, was just around the corner!

Let's face it, it was awesome being a suburban kid on the North Shore of Chicago and just eight years of age in 1958. I knew that I would have a great time taking my two puppies for a walk together on the west side of Glencoe. The Skokie Lagoons were mysterious, and I was anxious to check them out on my own. I could explore my independence, on my terms. Life, liberty and the pursuit of happiness were mine to enjoy!

After breakfast, I went into the kitchen, where I could see Mr. Chips and Schopenhauer were finishing up their breakfast bowls on the laundry room floor.

"Massa Jeffrey, you neez guh'n busy yuh'sef cuz I's gittin' lunch fuh yo mama 'n duh ladies," our wonderful Lo said, speaking in her cutely broken English and smiling her big Caribbean grin as Mr. Chips let out a bark and took off through the small 'pets' screen door at the kitchen back entrance, followed quickly by the clumsy golden retriever in sudden pursuit.

"Geh'bye, Show!" Lo exclaimed nonsensically as Schopenhauer squeezed himself through the swinging portal to canine freedom and disappeared in a flash.

"Hold on and wait for me, Schopenhauer!" I called out after him, then said to the maid, "see ya, Lo, be back later! Hey, Schopenhauer and Mr. Chips, wait for me!"

"Wha'abow' yo' breh'fiss, massa Jef?" Lo called out.

"It can wait!" I answered her.

The last thing I remembered after I ran out of the laundry room door was that I jumped off the concrete stoop at the back of the house, then I tripped and somersaulted into the tall impenetrable bush hedge between us and our neighbors before I blacked out for a minute, woke up quickly, heard my two puppies and their fading barks in the distance, then chased after them along our steeply descending driveway toward Skokie Ridge and the western edge of Glencoe.

I could see the two puppies scampering down Elm Ridge Drive, racing past the intersection with Skokie Ridge and then heading north and disappearing around the bend toward Sunset Lane; but I wasn't sure if they'd head north toward Greenbay Road or west toward Hohlfelder Road and the intriguing lagoons, so I called after them, "wait for me, you two; please stop!"

I continued crying out to them, but to no avail. Mr. Chips and his buddy Schopenhauer weren't having any of my exhortations to halt. They both scurried onward has if they had an important date or destination; but I had no idea where that might be. All I knew as I rounded the bend at Skokie Ridge was that I could see they were heading west toward the perimeter boundary of where I usually bicycled Hohlfelder Road. But I could tell that today, they were on a mission beyond our typical haunts. I wondered, where were my two puppies heading?

CHAPTER TWO: THE MYSTERIOUS SKOKIE LAGOONS

When I made it down Skokie Ridge and around the corner of Sunset Lane to Hohlfelder Road, I first looked north toward the Glencoe Municipal Golf Course and didn't see my two runaway puppies; but then I quickly looked south and saw Mr. Chips and Schopenhauer scamper around the northwest side corner of Hohlfelder Road and Dundee Road, where I watched in sheer amazement as they took off heading west along the north border of busy Dundee Road toward the overpass at the Skokie Lagoons.

"Hold on, you two! Where do you think you're both going without me?" I called out to Mr. Chips and Schopenhauer, who ignored me completely while continuing to race west along Dundee Road's northern border.

The sun was shining brightly, and it was a beautiful morning as cars whizzed by; but I wasn't paying any attention to the traffic or the kids' baseball game which was in full swing across the busy thoroughfare at newly constructed West School's athletic field. I could hear the cheers of the onlookers in the bleachers who were wrapped up in the latest hit out of the ballpark with bases loaded, handing a near certain victory to the home team. Yay for the kids at West School!

I, however, had no time to enjoy the accolades with kids from Strawberry Hill and the Ridges over in my part of town because Mr. Chips and Schopenhauer were about to disappear from my view in the hazy distance and glare of bright sunshine reflected off of the newly paved asphalt of Dundee Road.

CHAPTER THREE: THE NORTH BRANCH

"**M**r. Chips and Schopenhauer, wait for me!" I called out to my puppies once more as they dashed way ahead of me along the grassy north side of Dundee Road. I had darted from the corner of Hohlfelder Road and Dundee while looking westward toward Edens Highway; and it was in that direction and after I'd passed West School that I caught a glimpse of Mr. Chips and Schopenhauer as they approached the intervening Dundee Road overpass at the Skokie Lagoons, which was just east of and next to Edens Highway at Dundee Road.

Traffic continued to whiz ominously by me as I ran westward on the grassy border. I'd taken only a moment to check out the large crowd across the road at West School's sports event; but then I turned back toward the Dundee Road overpass to the west, where my two puppies had simply vanished into thin air.

Where could they be, I wondered? I was concerned that I'd lost them forever; but I didn't stop hoping I'd find them when I finally arrived at the overpass overlooking the lagoons.

I looked all around the roadway area's upper embankment where I'd last seen them; and there was no trace of them in the bushes along the side of the busy thoroughfare.

On a lark, I decided to traipse down and underneath the north side of the overpass, where I saw Mr. Chips and Schopenhauer boarding a flat floating crate about six feet square with a small jib and mainsail in the middle, both made of checkerboard tablecloths, like the ones at the nice Italian restaurant Mother liked, My Favorite Inn in Highwood.

There was a goofy flimsy looking Rube Goldberg-esque steering contraption on the back of the quirky crate made of an old wooden shovel that was attached in the center to the back of the crate with a metal vise and yet I could see that somehow it could be maneuvered ninety degrees in the water for direction because it was gently undulating from side to side in the languorous lagoon current. How ingeniously kooky the whole contraption looked, I thought! It reminded me of the raft that Tom Sawyer and Huckleberry Finn used on the Mississippi River, though this one was smaller and less seaworthy.

By this point, Schopenhauer and Mr. Chips were on board, wagging their tails and barking at me to join them on this journey of a lifetime to 'who knows where?'

I certainly didn't know; but I was willing to join my canine buddies and see where the mysterious drift of the labyrinthine lagoons would carry us. I could tell that Mr. Chips was the first mate when he barked to me to release the rope tied to a boulder on the side of the muddy bank where curious emerald colored frogs stared bleakly at us; and then the captain, Schopenhauer, manned the steering contraption as we shoved off into the middle of the murky purple stream just to the south of Dundee Road, where we enjoyed a wonderful view of the luxuriantly blooming and impenetrable woods on either side of the waterway as we wound our way through the twists and turns of the spooky Cook County forest preserve, where the stillness of late spring was broken only by an occasional murder of crows or murmuration of starlings.

As we approached the bridge over the lagoon waterway at Tower Road, located just to the east of Edens Highway in the forest preserve, I noticed a group of well wishers on the overpass waving pennants that read 'Go Mr. Chips!' and 'Right on Schopenhauer!' which I thought was odd because I hadn't told anybody about this unassuming sail of ours through the Skokie Lagoons. How could our anonymity possibly be discovered, I wondered?

"Wave back!" Mr. Chips barked, as he wagged his tail.

"Ok!" I responded, waving; and then I asked him, "wait a second! Did you just speak?"

"Of course he did, silly!" Schopenhauer answered, barking and smiling with his panting pink tongue glistening in the morning sun.

"Hold on just a second!" I said to my two puppies as we continued heading south under the bridge, "you guys have never talked before!"

They just silently wagged their tails, ignoring me, with Mr. Chips up front scouting the best way forward through the lakes of the lagoon and Schopenhauer steering in back of the makeshift barque as we floated through the jade waters which followed alongside Forest Way and the western edge of the Winnetka golf course under a dome of sky tinged an ethereal blue pink.

Funny that I didn't think it odd that my puppies had spoken to me, just unprecedented; but I didn't have time to focus on that anomaly because I suddenly remembered that there was a dam at Willow Road that separated the lagoon waterway from the Skokie River, where our cruise would naturally end at the spillway; but, as we approached the tunnel and lagoon junction with Willow Road, the dam was nowhere to be seen and that was most certainly strange!

"The water level must be very high today!" I said to my canine compatriots, who wagged their tails and barked, "because the dam underneath Willow Road has completely disappeared!" I said, startled into disbelief.

It was still early in the morning, but I couldn't figure out why the dome of sunshine above had suddenly turned sky blue, then pink; the lagoon water reflecting the clouds had changed from jade green to almond; while a large cloud bank shifted dark green.

And along the riverfront, the once blackened gray foliage became a dazzling mélange of cotton candy conifers, lollipop trees and chocolate scented bushes. How ridiculously odd, I thought, as I contemplated the rainbow-colored dreamscape of the surrounding lagoons through which we floated.

"Well, that's silly!" I said, adding, "the Contac allergy capsule I took this morning for my hay fever must be giving me these outrageous hallucinations!"

"Yes, that's it!" Schopenhauer barked.

"Did you just speak too?" I asked him as he wagged his tail and silently smiled while we passed right over the swirling storm drain and fast-moving waters of the tunnel under Willow

Road.

"I know that this is just impossible because I've read that the dam at Willow Road regulates the water level and amount of discharge into the downstream river!" I announced officiously, "so no boat bigger than a toy could slip through here without being stuck in the dam's breakwater!"

"Well not today because we're no bigger than toys ourselves!" Mr. Chips barked.

"That's meshuga because we can't just shrink or change shape on a whim!" I responded, forgetting for a moment that I was having a serious discussion with a puppy of mine.

"If you can imagine it, anything is possible!" Schopenhauer barked as we continued sailing south along the narrow stream winding through the forest preserve toward the underpass at Edens Highway, which was just south of Stepan Chemical, where I pointed at the headquarters on the west side of the busy commuter thoroughfare in the distance and said, "they're one of the premier manufacturers of surfactants in the world!" I announced confidently, taking pride in my unusual knowledge of chemicals as a precocious eight-year-old who glanced at The Wall Street Journal from time to time.

I was already a capitalist by then, earning a year's worth of interest on my small passbook savings account I'd opened at the Glencoe National Bank, as well as several quarterly dividend payments from the odd lot of IBM which Mother had generously gifted to me.

"There's the newly built Carson Pirie Scott Department Store in the mall!" I said to the two pooches, as we floated southwest past the Edens Shopping Center and then continued due south through the forest preserve toward the Nixon Woods and close enough to Hackneys in Glenview to smell their world-famous hamburgers cooking and being served alfresco on their outdoor patio at one of America's greatest and most charming suburban restaurant bars. I had often dreamt of their miniature hot fudge sundaes, the cutest little deserts imaginable, even for an eight-year-old kid who fondly remembered as a toddler enjoying a small taste of baked Alaska at his parents' dinner parties.

On and on we floated downstream, passing to the west of Old Orchard and then the delicatessens along Dempster and Touhy east of the Edens Expressway. It wasn't long before the river turned southeast as it flowed under the highway just to the north of Edens junction and overpass at Cicero Avenue.

And it was there that I remembered that the world famous Affy Tapple store on North Clark was a good distance further east and perhaps just a smidgen south. I so missed not being able to stop there and hoped to return to that famous confectioner someday; but there was a place coming up along the river that was just as unforgettable and I couldn't wait to see its spires and domes, its roller coasters and pennants fluttering in the breeze.

I could smell the popcorn and freshly made cotton candy long before I saw the place, looking like a vision of the ancient city of Samarkand to a boy of eight steeped in the bedtime stories of 1001 Arabian Nights. It was an amusement park unlike any other I'd ever seen; so much so that I'd even dreamt of it. Who could ever forget the magnificent and unique Riverview?

CHAPTER FOUR: RIVERVIEW PARK

As our makeshift raft sailed along the Chicago River toward Riverview, the most amazing amusement park in America, I asked Mr. Chips and Schopenhauer if we could stop, tie up nearby along the shoreline and visit my favorite place in the whole world.

"Why, sure!" the two of them barked in unison. Well, that was surprisingly easy, I thought.

We three moored our craft behind Aladdin's Castle and scrambled up the muddy weed strewn embankment. My puppies were far more surefooted on the littered and unkempt slope along the riverfront than I; but before long, we found ourselves at the entrance to the famed park, where there just happened to be a small mobile bodega selling Affy Tapples, of all things, with an old guy who had a huge bunch of multicolored balloons tied to a corner of his wheeled cart. I remembered seeing this guy before; and I tried to place him from wherever it was I'd seen him. Then I recollected where it had been.

"You look exactly like the fortune teller Dorothy meets at the beginning of the movie of The Wizard of Oz!" I announced.

"Well, I think you're speaking of Frank Morgan, though that's just a happy happenstance, young man; but I assure you and your two canine friends, I'm just another old carny from Kansas who happens to be selling balloons and these delicious caramel coated apples for a little supplemental income!" he stated proudly. "Sometimes I'm here and other times I'm along Sheridan Road several blocks south of the Baha'I Temple—!"

"Yes, my stepfather has bought balloons from you there when I've accompanied him to Wyler Hospital on occasion!" I interrupted the old guy.

"Now I remember you!" the kindly old man responded, "but tell me, who have we here with you?" he asked, looking over at my two cute puppies.

"Mr. Chips and Schopenhauer!" I answered, "and I'm Jeff. We three are out for a fun day of exploring the city before we head home for dinner," I added as he handed me a complimentary Affy Tapple and gave each of the puppies a tasty puppy biscuit which they gobbled instantaneously.

I thanked the friendly old guy profusely and then my puppies barked their appreciation.

"Goodbye you three! Goodbye Mr. Chips! Goodbye Schopenhauer!" the old carny called out in his melodious voice as we departed his cute rolling cart with the red and white striped awning.

We next approached the front gates of the famous Riverview Amusement Park, where a ticket selling booth was located and a friendly looking older man dressed up as Uncle Sam was sitting and helping young people in line.

"What can I do for you and your two canine friends today?" he asked of me when we arrived at the head of the line.

"I know I can't bring them in—!" I said, nearly stammering.

"Why!" he interrupted me, "surely you can today, young fella, it's the Riverview Ramble and all are welcome!" he said positively joyously.

"Well, you never allowed this before, on the Ramble or any other day!" I answered seriously.

"Today I'm making an exception!" the old man said, as Mr. Chips and Schopenhauer barked their approval.

A dark cloud bank passed from in front of the sun, the sky turned a bright pink and then powder blue; and when I looked up, I thought I saw a giant eye where the sun had been, and then it disappeared in a flash, melting back into the intense yellow orb.

What was going on here, I wondered? And why, for goodness' sake, did the kindly old man at the front gate allow me in with Mr. Chips and Schopenhauer in tow? I knew of course that that was without precedent; but, for the time being I thought no further of it; and, with three tickets in my hand, we marched into the famous amusement park.

"What do you boys think?" I asked of Mr. Chips and Schopenhauer as they pranced officiously, barked in unanimous approval and then both took a sip from a gleaming pewter colored water bowl conveniently situated on the ground next to the front entrance drinking fountain.

"Let's see all the highfalutin' rollercoasters!" I said as we made our way along the north side of the park. To me, they were the greatest roller coasters ever. There were always long lines of kids waiting to board the Bobs, the Comet and the Silver Flash and the day's crowds were no different.

I knew that such rides, as well as the Shoot the Chutes and the Flying Turns, weren't appropriate for my puppies; but they were great to see in action, even if we couldn't enjoy them. But there was one amusement we three could enjoy, the mysterious Aladdin's Castle, with all its twisty turns and secret hidden passages; and we were heading that way as we walked by the pair-o'-chutes, a neat parachute ride.

"Sorry, Mr. Chips and Schopenhauer, the roller coasters and other thrill rides are just too dangerous for you both and me too; but we can go to Aladdin's Castle if you want!" I said, as they barked in the affirmative and in unison.

"Step right up with your tickets for the castle!" said the gaudily dressed barker in the garb of a flamboyant clown.

"After this ride, we must get back on the river!" I told my two happy puppies in a very serious tone, while noting the oddity of their being granted access into the castle when I knew full well that that was definitely not kosher, even if it was safe. But precedence or not, we three had a wonderful time going through all the twists and turns of the place, a maze of mirrors and skeletons, goblins and ghouls that frightened the crowds of kids who packed into the place with us that afternoon.

"It's time for us to return to our little skiff on the river!" I said to Mr. Chips and Schopenhauer when we exited the castle through a trap door and squinted in the bright sunshine of a gorgeous Chicago spring day.

Our little barque awaited our return; yet, when I looked south and east and saw the Morton Salt warehouse along the Chicago and Northwestern Railroad tracks, I realized that we were way past Irving Park and a quick jaunt over to Wrigley field, where we could have seen a Cubs doubleheader, enjoyed the most delicious steamed hotdogs with a dollop of mustard in the whole world and then taken the famous 'El' after the game from the Addison Street station all the way back home to Glencoe and Park Avenue.

"I'm sorry guys that you'll miss the 'dogs' at Wrigley Field!" I laughed at the play on words as they looked at me with a quizzical expression and turn of their heads, "but just perhaps I can get you on a part of that journey!" I said arcanely. And I knew just how to do it too, without revealing the big surprise I'd planned.

We boarded our little wooden crate vessel with the patchwork fabric sails and set off down the Chicago River, passing Clybourn and Division, where old factories and ramshackle buildings were interspersed with famous landmarks like the Morton Salt warehouse and the huge old Montgomery Ward complex. What a thrill it was to see these wonderfully decrepit old buildings from the silent perspective of cruising down the Chicago River!

CHAPTER FIVE: MORTON SALT

As we floated by the Morton Salt warehouse, I suddenly realized my sense of direction had been messed up by my greater wish for adventure; and while it was great being able to show my puppies the thrills of Riverview, we'd gone way beyond the Addison Street bridge, which was where I'd wanted to disembark to go see the Cubs play at Wrigley Field over by the "El" tracks near Halsted Street.

"Boys!" I said to Mr. Chips and Schopenhauer, "we may have missed our disembarkation point at Addison awhile back and before Riverview, but I've got a plan to get us back on track for the Cubs game today, if you're still with me!" I announced confidently to loud barks of approval from both of my canine companions.

"We can't easily backtrack up the Chicago River; but if we continue to float down toward the confluence with the south branch of the river at the Merchandise Mart, I have an idea that will still get us to the Cubs and Wrigley Field by the time of the first pitch. I'll need you guys to help me steer and catch the wind in our makeshift sails if we're going to pull this off. So, Schopenhauer, man the steering contraption; and Mr. Chips, let out the jib and mainsail a little to catch the breeze coming from the northwest!" I said as a gust of wind pushed us south past Division Street.

The downtown city skyline came into view as we floated under the bridges at Grand and Illinois Avenues before we approached the majestic merging of both branches of the great river where the jewel in the crown of the city center held court, the magnificent and immense Merchandise Mart, one of the most impressive buildings in the world. Just north of Chicago's spectacular city "Loop", so named because of the elevated train tracks encircling it, the setting of 'The Mart' to the north of the downtown buildings along the river was utterly awe inspiring to a kid with an interest in art and architecture.

Lake Michigan glittered to the east of downtown, a vast carpet of sapphires dancing in the sunlight beyond the Chicago River entrance; and I was in heaven and floating dockside with my two favorite puppies as we got ready to tie up our little sailing craft at the Franklin Street bridge.

CHAPTER SIX:
THE 'EL'

"**C**'mon boys!" I called out to Mr. Chips and Schopenhauer, both of whom scrambled out of the little sailboat and trotted after me along the concrete pier and up the steps to where the staircase for the 'el' train was located next to the famed Merchandise Mart.

"Hurry up or we'll miss the next 'El' heading north from the loop!" I called out as the clattering train noisily crossed the bridge at the Chicago River on its approach to our stop.

It was a breeze getting three tickets for us and we crowded onto the first open car that stopped in front of us at the platform. The east side of the Mart cast the train and us inside of it in heavy shadow; but as the train pulled away from the station, sunlight poured through the smudged windows and onto the crowds of people talking and petting Mr. Chips and Schopenhauer, who were incredibly well behaved and easily able to balance themselves on the swaying and bumpy old 'El' train despite all the good natured kvelling heaped upon them.

I didn't mind the inconvenience of those on the train who found Mr. Chips and Schopenhauer irresistible though because I was thrilled to be able to show my puppies how special a day it would be at Wrigley Field with the Cubs at home and the hotdogs steaming fresh! Life could be perfect at eight years of age! Mine certainly was because of my puppies, my city and our ride on the 'El' to see our favorite baseball team at the famed ivy-covered stadium!

CHAPTER SEVEN: THE CUBS

It wasn't long before the clattering train made the several-mile journey from River North at the Merchandise Mart stop. It was a glorious day as we passed Belmont Harbor and then Diversey Harbor to the east. The sun shone upon Lake Michigan, turning it into an endless golden carpet of amethyst and aquamarine sparkling beneath a pale blue crystal sky as the 'El' rattled into the Addison Street station.

We disembarked at the station by Wrigley Field and scampered down the dark stairwell to the busy street as buses and cars whizzed by in a whirlwind of gas fumes and honking, startling my two puppies into crowding near me on their leashes.

"Now, you two, you stay right by me!" I admonished them as I looked up and stared at the panoramic Addison Street scene before me, comprising the marvelously curved and awe-inspiring Wrigley Stadium.

"There it is, boys!" I said, "one of the most famous baseball parks in all the world, Wrigley Field!"

Mr. Chips and Schopenhauer wagged their tails as I tightened their leashes before crossing the busy street corner by the ballpark.

"Let's go see Ernie Banks and check out Jack Brickhouse and Lou Boudreau up in the announcer's booth!" I said of the famous baseball player and the two locally well-known television and radio personalities who were nearly always present for the Cubs games at Wrigley, along with the owner, the legendary chewing gum magnate, Mr. Wrigley.

We were able to get three bleachers seats for a song that day because it was hot and humid; and what a wonderful day it was, including a bright blue sky filled with loads of sunshine and cute little powder puff clouds lazily floating by the field, as if they too were in no particular hurry to miss any of the excitement going on down below during game warmup.

"I know I don't have to ask if you boys want any steamed frankfurters and A&W root beer!" I said to Mr. Chips and Schopenhauer after we got to a bench high up at the very top of the bleachers, where we were seated virtually all by ourselves in the perfectly warm sun.

When the hotdog vendor carrying the aromatic metal chest of steamed treats came up to see us before the game started, I told him I only had a dollar for food and a dollar for the 'El' back home and he gave us the delicious, wrapped hotdogs, mine loaded with 'the works', as well as three drinks, all for a buck. I think he was being pretty darn nice to us because it should have cost more than that; but Mr. Chips and Schopenhauer were so cute, I think that the old guy couldn't resist their canine charms.

"Why is there a tear running down your cheek, Sir?" I asked him as he handed me the drinks.

"It must be that the wind blew something in my eye," he responded, smiling; but I didn't believe him because I knew that I and my two canine buddies were pretty cool all right, doggone it!

"Thank you, Sir!" I called after him as he descended the bleacher stairs to the crowds below and turned around once more to look at us with another tear still in his eye.

I didn't know what he saw that made him appear sad. I just knew that I wasn't, and not on such a perfect day as this with my two best buddies in the whole world!

"We're gonna see Ernie Banks today, boys!" I said as the two puppies finished their plain frankfurter meals and joined me on the bleachers to watch the exciting practice and pregame activity on the field.

It wasn't long before the game started, and the Cubs were first at bat. A few minutes later, I couldn't believe my good fortune in seeing Lee Walls, Tony Taylor and Dale Long that day. A short while further in the inning and with bases loaded, Ernie Banks came up to bat, spit on the mound and readied himself, then waited what seemed like an eternity for the pitch from the Phillies' pitcher, Don Cardwell, who threw strike one, then threw a fast ball causing Banks to foul strike two up into the bleachers above first base, with the ball landing serendipitously a few yards from me. Before I could believe my good fortune, Schopenhauer instinctively and quickly scrambled to pick up the ball before the kids sitting several rows below us could grab it.

"Good boy, Schope!" I said, as Schopenhauer returned to me and the television cameras caught me waving the hall in the air with Jack Brickhouse announcing, "now that's a lucky kid today, folks!"

Yes indeed, but it would get better because after that perfect foul, the third pitch from Cardwell resulted in Ernie Banks hitting a home run right on out of the park with those bases loaded, a truly magnificent sight at my favorite baseball stadium, whose well-manicured ivy-covered walls, a Wrigley Field trademark, were no match for Mr. Banks batting prowess.

The Cubs would go on to trounce the Phillies; and after the game, I took Mr. Chips and Schopenhauer on leashes to the expensive seats over by the dugout, where I politely asked Mr. Banks if he'd autograph the ball of his which the television cameras filmed that day. And of course, he agreed, thank goodness, just like in a dream.

"Thank you, Mr. Banks!" I said, as Mr. Chips and Schopenhauer barked their approval in convivial concord.

"It's time we three catch the "El" north to home!" I said to my two puppies.

"Where's that, young man?" Mr. Banks asked solicitously, looking at Schopenhauer and Mr. Chips, who were simultaneously pulling on their leashes, as if to say, 'let's go!'

"Why, Glencoe, Sir, where I live with my parents, brother Alec and sister Sharon!"

"You take care of yourself, young man!" Mr. Banks said kindly as I took off for the 'El' station with my puppies and my prize possession, Mr. Banks' spectacularly autographed baseball.

By now, the front of the park was quiet, the earlier crowds had dispersed, and we climbed the metal stairs at the Addison Street station for the oncoming noisy old train heading north. It had been a perfect day!

In the flash of a moment, the train screeched to a halt, we boarded, got seats and were on our way to the North Shore and home; but before that, I had one more stop along the route which I wanted Mr. Chips and Schopenhauer to see up close, the world-famous Baha'I temple across Sheridan Road from the picturesque Wilmette Harbor.

"I have a special treat for you two to visit before we get back home!" I told my puppies, who looked at me with quizzical expressions. "You'll just have to wait and see!" I said, "that's all there is to it, boys!"

I could tell that Mr. Chips and Schopenhauer were excited because they sat on the train seat next to me and stared out the windows as we clattered northbound from Addison Street, stopping at many local stations along the route, from Uptown and the Gold Coast neighborhoods to Roger's Park and Northwestern, before arriving at the Wilmette station, where we disembarked at Linden Street a couple blocks west of the world famous Baha'I Temple.

CHAPTER EIGHT: THE BAHA'I TEMPLE

"C'mon boys!" I called out to my puppies after we departed from the 'El' station, "let me take you to a very special place!" I said, as we started walking east on Linden Street toward Sheridan Road and Lake Michigan, where the magnificent Baha'I Temple was located, across from the Wilmette Harbor and beautiful Gillson Park, its trees showing off large green canopies of bright green leaves for spring.

"There it is, boys!" I called out enthusiastically, blown away by the dramatic structure appearing like the top three quarters of a gigantic Faberge egg nestled into the large rounded earthen mound of geometrically designed formal gardens. The temple building shone in the setting sun, with it's incredible and intricately carved concrete filigree work, a marvel of stunning architectural majesty in its lofty Wilmette lakefront location, where many Frank

Lloyd Wright residential masterpieces graced the surrounding suburban landscape with equally impressive grandeur.

"Boys, we don't have time to see the famous Wright designed house in Wilmette and a few blocks northwest of here; but perhaps I'll be able to take you there soon!" I exclaimed, as my two puppies wagged their tails in polite agreement.

I walked Mr. Chips and Schopenhauer through the gorgeously manicured gardens that were designed in a starburst pattern and appearing as if their colors were emanating from the very temple itself, a magical effect of flowers that fit neatly within the circular temple property which bordered the curve of Sheridan Road to the east and north, the North Shore Channel to the west and Linden Street to the south.

"We have to be on our very best behavior here at the Baha'I Temple, boys!" I said to my independent minded puppies, "remember that the only thing you can do on the grounds of the temple is smell the flowers and nothing more!" I admonished them seriously.

Looking at me quizzically, my puppies weren't crazy about not being permitted to leave their unique calling cards, just as any respectable pooch would want to do; but I said to them, "we must be respectful here! Don't worry, boys, we won't tarry here too long. You'll have plenty of opportunities on the walk back along Linden to furnish your inestimable identification. But let's also remember, we have to make sure that we are home for dinner or Mother will be worried about us!" I continued, as Mr. Chips and Schopenhauer quietly sniffed all the pretty flower borders and did nothing more.

It wasn't long before I'd shown them the remarkably sparse interior of the astonishing temple. We were able to deferentially peer into the light filled sanctuary from the temple's open doors; and I could glean from their puzzled looks that neither of them could figure out what all the fuss was about here. Surprisingly, the holy place was practically devoid of ornamentation inside. But I knew that that was the point of it all, after all. Some religions had incredibly gaudy interiors resplendent with some of the greatest artistic masterpieces in the western world; but for the followers of Baha'I, the interior space was reserved for their reverence, quiet contemplation and personal spiritual observance, not a vulgar display of lurid grandeur and excessive religious spectacle. You could tell that there was no pomposity here. The interior was awe inspiring in its spareness of detail; and I knew that I'd never know a more restrained or better example of what a great house of worship should look like than the Baha'I Temple of Wilmette.

****
***

By the time we made it back to the Linden Street 'El' station, it was the perfect moment to catch the upcoming North Shore train departing Wilmette for Glencoe and home. I had had a wonderful day with my puppies and now it was time to call it a day.

"Thank you both for coming with me on my adventure in the big city!" I said to Mr. Chips and Schopenhauer, who wagged their tails in grateful friendship and barked their approval of a doggone fun day out on the town.

My two puppies were too kind to not remind me that it was I, however, who had accompanied them on the day's fantastic journey; and not the other way around.

CHAPTER NINE: BACK HOME TO GLENCOE

"Ok, boys, get ready to catch the next train on the North Shore Line from Linden to Glencoe!" I said, as the rickety old streetcar came into view. "We'll be able to enjoy one more train ride home today!"

By this point, the clattering streetcar had ground to a stop and we three climbed aboard as I dropped the right amount of coins into the engineer's hopper, after which I found us a bench where we could all sit together and watch the view as we passed from Wilmette through Winnetka, then Hubbard Woods and on into my hometown of Glencoe, whose station was located just north of Park Avenue. What a wonderful day it had been with my two cute canine buddies, Mr. Chips and Schopenhauer!

By the time we arrived back at the Park Avenue station in Glencoe, my little cranky schnauzer and happy-go-lucky golden retriever were all too thrilled to be ambling off of the North Shore streetcar with me in the lead.

It was a clear sky of robin's eggshell blue overhead darkening to sapphire toward the east in the dim light of the late afternoon sun, with Lake Michigan sparkling a deep gray shade of jade through spots in the malachite-colored tree canopy lining both sides of Park Avenue. Little pink powderpuff clouds dyed apricot pewter underneath from the setting sun were drifting slowly above the church just east of the train station, where a congregation of old oak and maple trees were handsomely dressed and ready for Sunday's upcoming and well-advertised ice cream social. A mischief of hidden magpies was squawking belligerently within the trees' full spring canopies, their bright green foliage surrounding the church shimmering in the softly iridescent late afternoon light.

It would have been nice to head east of the tracks, past the ancient church and over to the beach; but I'd had enough excitement for one afternoon and my puppies were ready for their dinner as well as a good night's rest after a long day filled with our many delightful adventures.

It was time to be homeward bound now for me and my puppies as I patiently waited for an express commuter passenger train to whiz by on the Chicago and Northwestern tracks which ran parallel to the North Shore streetcar line we'd just disembarked from. A huge cloud of dust was kicked up by the train roaring by as I looked at the rapidly disappearing rounded club car at the back of the commuter express until it vanished in the hazy sunshine reflected off the tracks by North School, which I attended, where 'Miss 'Ole Larceny' was our humorously nicknamed teacher.

Sometimes I thought she was a real pretty doll; but other times, I wasn't too fond of her. In any case, I was relieved I didn't have to see Miss Larse, that old prig and wind bag, for a whole summer of vacation. She was one big 'ugh' of a teacher and occasionally reminded me of the famous sitting portrait of Gertrude Stein by Pablo Picasso, especially when Miss Larse was sitting in her chair at the head of our class instructing us.

"Cmon boys, let's trot along Park Avenue into the village and see what's going on in downtown Glencoe before we head home!" I said, as the traffic light turned from red to green at Greenbay Road and we crossed the street, walking along Park Avenue past the stately maroon brick library and Fell's Clothing store on the south side and Mr. Ricky's Delicatessen and the Glencoe National Bank on the north side. We then approached the Old Surprise Shop, the cutest little toy store in the whole world.

I stopped and stared at all the wonderful toys and games in the windows while Mr. Chips and Schopenhauer dutifully and quietly sat as passersby paused and petted them; one of whom, a distinguished older matron, announced, "it looks like a scene just made for Norman Rockwell, what with you and your two puppies!" she gushed. It was Mrs. Letitia Hight, one of our neighbors on Elm Ridge Drive.

I was too busy to thank her, a sweet lady, because I was utterly mesmerized and consumed by the treasure filled windows before me, a scene overflowing with knickknacks and gewgaws, gimcracks and surprise balls, toys, games and puzzles, miniature cars and trains in all manner of profusion throughout the store and overflowing around the bay window scenes. I didn't pay attention to any of the onlookers or shoppers because the front door to the legendary toy emporium swung open to reveal an old friend I'd known and adored since I was barely a toddler.

CHAPTER TEN: THE OLD SURPRISE SHOP

"Why, Mr. Vetch, won't you and your puppies come in and please see our latest arrivals?" Miss Prim, the toy store proprietress, graciously asked in a softly mellifluous tone, her librarian's voice barely above a whisper as she handed Mr. Chips and Schopenhauer each a puppy biscuit and put down a gleaming pewter bowl filled with sparkling water which the pair quickly imbibed. How odd, I thought, that that bowl matched the one at Riverview earlier, like in a repetitive dream.

"Mind your manners in front of the lady, gentlemen!" I instructed my puppies, who tempered their mutual enthusiasm for the libation long enough to bark their enthusiastic agreement.

"We really should be getting home, Miss Prim!" I stated unconvincingly, not believing a word of what I was wanly stating.

"You can have your pick of any of the gorgeous softball sized surprise balls overflowing in the large barrel just inside the front door, and with my compliments, of course, Jeffrey; and you can bring in your canine companions too!" she announced, an iconoclastic break with the infamously strict rules against any pets of any kind in her store, ever!

"Well, perhaps I and the boys can peruse your little bodega," I announced seriously, trying to sound very sophisticated for my age.

"You have quite a vocabulary for such a young man!" Miss Prim stated, as several passersby looked in through the opened front door at the extraordinary sight of me with Mr. Chips and Schopenhauer in a store famous for its strict adherence heretofore to the 'no pet' policy.

I could tell from Miss Prim's silent stares at the onlookers that this scene was the exception proving the rule that, in general, the 'no pets' policy still existed as the Surprise Shop mantra, irrespective of my specific treatment. And it wasn't my presence as much as the effect which Mr. Chips and Schopenhauer had on adult onlookers as they passed the legendary toy store's charming bay windows. They simply melted the most intransigent and jaded of hearts with their winning personalities.

While the elderly passersby continued

kvelling over my adorable puppies, I looked over all the toys in the charming shop, including a miniature electric battery operated Rolls Royce Corniche convertible with a remote radio controller which was large enough for a very small boy; but that inconvenience didn't stop Mr. Chips from jumping into the driver's seat, flipping the battery switch to 'on' and driving around the store manually like a manic, to the utter amazement of Miss Prim, who was stunned into silent stupefaction while Schopenhauer clumsily chased Mr. Chips in his little Rolls all around the place.

"Ok, boys, we best say thank you to Miss Prim and be on our way!" I said firmly as Mr. Chips roared to a stop with Schopenhauer clumsily crashing into the back of the little Rolls, shaking himself off and then galumphing out the front door.

"Goodbye Schopenhauer!" I called out to him as Miss Prim handed me a baseball-sized 'Surprise Ball' with little gimcracks and gewgaws hidden and wrapped inside its multicolored ribbons.

"Goodbye you three!" Miss Prim responded, waving at us.

"We'll stop by again soon!" I called out to her as we dashed out of the store and skipped along the sidewalk west past the famous Glencoe establishment, Miller's Delicatessen, its bespoke sign shimmering in the late afternoon sun across the busy street, Park Avenue. We then headed west from the corner of Vernon Avenue as the pale gray clouds and the pink apricot setting sunlight filtered through the smoky haze of the late afternoon; and with my puppies in tow, we approached the corner at Bluff Street.

The sun had by now turned dusky rose orange in the faded gray sky over the bluff; and the clouds' merged silhouettes were indistinguishable, one from the other, in the gauzy early evening light, reflecting an impressionist chiaroscuro sky more akin to a Pissarro painting than an actual sunset. Yet it was an actual sky; and I could feel the effect its inenarrable ambience had upon me without being able to enunciate it, even at eight years of age in the glorious year of 1958.

"C'mon, guys, we have to hurry!" I said to my puppies, "you don't want to be late for your dinner, now do you, Mr. Chips and Schopenhauer?" I asked them as we scampered north on Bluff Road toward Dundee Road and the last leg of our journey back home, after a perfectly wonderful day filled with adventures only a little boy and his puppies could appreciate.

CHAPTER ELEVEN: RETURNING HOME

After we crossed Dundee Road, Mr. Chips and Schopenhauer pulled me along with them on their leashes as fast as they could; and we ran west along the busy thoroughfare a short distance before cutting through a couple of neighbors' properties on the north side of Dundee Road before skirting a small ravine area separating several of our Elm Ridge Drive backyards, where bluebells grew in the Lilliputian valley and butterflies fluttered amongst ancient pines whose limbs gavotted in the light breezes of the early evening; and just when we dashed through our backyard's intervening lilac hedge sporting its aromatic soft purple flowers and crossed the tan bark by my older brother Alec's kid-sized log cabin, I coincidentally tripped over the border log separating the tan bark from the grass over by the laundry room back door where I'd tripped on its concrete step earlier that very same day at the beginning of our morning adventure.

****

I must have blacked out once again because, when I awakened in my bedroom, my whole family was surprisingly there with me; and they were sitting next to me upon my bed and all around it on chairs as well as on my low-rise built-in toy cabinets underneath the windowsill.

"We weren't sure you were gonna make it for a while," Alec said, a tear welling up in his eyes.

"I had quite an adventure today!" I exclaimed.

"Sure, you did, son!" my stepfather Adolph said, sounding unconvinced about my story yet simultaneously disconsolate and relieved, nonetheless.

"You've been out for quite some time!" Mother said solemnly.

"I have, like ten minutes, right?" I asked.

"We're glad you're feeling better, young man!" the married couple of Paul, the chauffeur and Carol, the cook, chimed in simultaneously from the doorway of my bedroom.

"Mr. Chips, Schopenhauer and I traveled on

a small crate which the puppies made, complete with a makeshift mainsail and jib; and we floated all the way through the Skokie Lagoons from the Dundee Road embankment just east of the Edens Highway and then right from the Skokie River to the Chicago River North Branch, where we stopped first at Riverview Amusement Park and then the Merchandise Mart.

"Mr. Chips, Schopenhauer and I disembarked from our little sailing vessel and took the Franklin Street 'El' up to Wrigley Field and the Cubs game, where I ended up winning a ball hit by Mr. Banks that he autographed just for me; after which we then headed up north on the 'El' to the Baha'I Temple to look around at the place before catching the North Shore Line streetcar at Linden Street up to Glencoe and a quick stop at the Surprise Shop with Miss Prim before we three dashed north to home on Bluff, honest Injun!" I proclaimed proudly.

"That's quite an adventure you had!" Mother said, winking at Paul and Carol, "now you go and get some rest please, Jeffrey Joseph!" Mother said, sounding quite serious, "you've been out for quite some time! We'll check in on you later with some dinner and a beverage," she added as everyone quietly departed my bedroom and I nodded off, quite tired from my day's activities while my dear sweet sister Sharon remained my sole companion by my bedside.

CHAPTER TWELVE: AN EXPLANATION

"I know you believe me because there's my softball from Ernie Banks!" I said, having reawakened to see the last of my family to remain, my dear sister, Sharon, who was staring beatifically at me and then at the baseball Schopenhauer had gotten for me. I was so proud of that ball that I hadn't even noticed what was nestled right behind it in the shadows of the early evening.

"So, Sharon, darling?" I asked her, "please tell me—!"

"Do I have to?" she interrupted and queried me plaintively.

"Yes!" I requested, "yes you do, dear sister of mine, tell me, what really happened to me that caused me to black out and for how long too please, dear sweet sister of mine?"

With tears streaming down her gorgeous

ME AND MISTER CHIPS

face and her long shimmering golden brown hair cascading around her neck like ribbons of spun gold, she begged me, "don't make me burst your bubble, Jeffrey, honey!"

"Please!" I responded.

"Fact is, I got that baseball for you from Mr. Banks after your story made the local news!—-"

"You mean my adventure?" I interrupted her.

"No, dear, you're being, shall we say, out of commission, darling!"

"Why would my five minutes of fainting make the local news, Sharon? That's a bit of a stretch, don't you think?" I asked her.

"It must have been a slow news cycle and you trying to chase after your puppies was viewed as a human-interest story after our pediatrician Dr. Rambler mentioned your situation while being interviewed on WGN concerning the extraordinary effectiveness of the polio vaccines.

"Anyway, after that story aired on local television and while I was at Wrigley Field sitting by the Cubs dugout, I happened to see Mr. Banks standing right there! I called out to him and, amazingly, I had the opportunity to tell him who I was and also about you and lo and behold, there's your baseball, autographed and gifted from Mr. Banks to me for you, believe it or not!

"But frankly, Jeffrey, the story you've told us today about your adventures with Mr. Chips and Schopenhauer sailing down the Skokie Lagoons is so perfectly beautiful for an eight-year-old boy, why you should write it down someday! And please don't make me try and convince you of the pedestrian truth of how that baseball arrived on your nightstand! Just believe your fairytale and write the novella someday, dear.

"The truth, whatever that is, is far less appealing than the fairytale you've weaved from your vivid imagination, so please, whatever you do or think, please darling don't believe me!" Sharon said lovingly. "Don't make me repeat exactly what happened to you the day of your fall, dear. What's the difference?" she asked.

"Because I want to know, honey!" I stated firmly.

"If you insist, it was a few days ago, perhaps a week or so, when you ran out the back door of the house by the laundry room in pursuit of your puppies, you slipped on the concrete stair step, tripped and fell into the neighbor's bushes and were out for long enough that the pediatrician, Dr. Rambler, was quite concerned about you!" she said.

"How is ole' Rambles doing around the corner and down Sunset Lane?" I asked Sharon, while sitting up in bed.

"He's fine and he was just here too, right before you awakened. We found your puppies coincidentally in their front yard the day you fainted. We're all so glad you're better and awake after a week of family worries. Mother will be bringing you some dinner soon. Just rest dear!" Sharon said, kissing me on the forehead and quietly departing the way a perfect older sister would. Wow, was she a knockout!

****

After Sharon and everyone else had departed my small bedroom, I stared out the window at Elm Ridge Drive; and it was then when a ray of sunshine lit up a small snow globe behind where the baseball had been resting before Sharon moved it. Perhaps my older sister left me the snow globe as another present on her way out the door. I knew it had to be her. It was such a 'Sharon' sort of thing to do. I just simply adored her!

When I picked up the clear orb to study it, sure enough there was an image I remembered so well from my day's adventure, the one Sharon believed was just a fairytale. Well, whether it was a dream or not which I had recalled, inside the little crystalline globe was the unforgettable miniature scene of the minarets and spires beyond the famous entrance to Riverview Amusement Park;

and I could see in the glass orb where a tiny boy and his two equally minuscule canine friends were standing and looking at the famed park's front entrance.

I knew that that little boy was naturally me; and of course, those two puppies were Mr. Chips, my German schnauzer, and Schopenhauer, my golden retriever. They were the two best friends a little boy could have, waking or dreaming.

As I stared at Sharon's adorable gift, I said, "hi Mr. Chips!" to the little German schnauzer in the snow globe just as my golden retriever Schopenhauer trotted into my bedroom, barked and scampered out abruptly without so much as a 'by your leave'!

"Goodbye, Schopenhauer!" I called out to him and then put the little snow globe back onto my nightstand.

A cloud must have passed in front of the sun because both the sky and my bedroom darkened momentarily, as coincidentally did the scene in the snow globe; but just then I looked up through my bedroom windows to witness the majesty of the gathering gloaming and shimmering moon, tinted a pale sapphire; and I knew I'd never forget that wonderful amusement park, Riverview, or the fun times I had there with my two best friends in the whole world, Mr. Chips and Schopenhauer.

I don't know if my adventures that day really happened or I imagined it all, but the memories are just as sweet in either case. So, I'll end this little tale by saying to my puppies, Mr. Chips and Schopenhauer, 'good night to you both, my soulmates!'

Good night to you too and may all your dreams come true!

BOOK II: MISTER CHIPS AND BLUEBERRY

INTRODUCTION

Summer Vacation 1958

Transcribed From Jeff Vetch's childhood diary.\

Let me take a moment to introduce you to the narrator of a small story I wrote when I was very young. The narrator, you see, was me! And I was just a kid way back in 1958 and living in Glencoe on the North Shore of Chicago. I remember the events of that summer like it was yesterday because I wrote them down in a diary I'd been given as a gift, along with a blue teddy bear.

They were two wonderful presents from my Uncle Harold and Aunt Mona the previous Thanksgiving. Those precious gifts meant the world to me!

Unfortunately, by the spring, I had regrettably lost my favorite cute blue teddy bear and I desperately wanted to find him.

As it happened, the events I wrote down in my miniature diary all began on a typical tranquil warm day in late spring when I was out in our backyard with my brother and sister and some of our friends. But they weren't the only ones outside that day. No, we were also outback with our many animal friends too, including my puppies, Mr. Chips and Schopenhauer, who would eventually appear in others of my stories; as well as our pet rabbit, Gopher, who was always smartly dressed by my older brother; and let's not forget my older sister's cute little puppy, Snowball; as well as the neighbor's rascally cat, Oodles; and, last but not least, our friendly and adorable auburn haired neighborhood squirrel, the curmudgeonly Johnnie Raggedy Tail.

I could tell you what I remember happened next that afternoon, all those years ago when I misplaced my teddy bear, Blueberry, during our hectic game of croquet on the backyard lawn out next to our house's sunroom; but I think it best if I open my diary from the spring of '58 and share with you what I wrote as a kid back then, when I was very very young.

While you may find it hard to believe that an eight-year-old can not only read adult literature but write eruditely as well and even keep a detailed journal of reflections, it's a fact that some of us precocious kids could engage in those endeavors; and, of course, I was one such gifted boy. After all, Mozart wrote his first little symphony at five! Anyway, I hope you like my childhood diary's revelations, as well as my additional annotations sprinkled liberally throughout the text from an older and more contemporary perspective!

CHAPTER ONE: MY DIARY AT EIGHT YEARS OLD

Hi! I'm Jeff, I'm a kid and I'm very *very* smart for my age, just like my older brother Alec and my gorgeous older sister Sharon. I'm a precocious dreamer of fairytales I invent and I'm just eight years old! I live on Elm Ridge Drive in Glencoe. It's 1958 and my older sister Sharon and I each have a puppy; actually, I have two. My two are Mr. Chips and Schopenhauer while hers is Snowball. My older brother Alec has a pet rabbit whom he dresses up in very smart English outfits.

My tiny puppy, Mr. Chips, is a gray German schnauzer who looks old but is young, just like me. My big puppy Schopenhauer is a galumphing golden retriever. Sharon's puppy, Snowball, is a pure white toy Pomeranian. And Alec's rabbit is a goofball named Gopher. Gopher is the most stylish rabbit in our neighborhood. He's always dressed up fancily, like he's going to attend a business meeting or an afternoon tea.

****

I was given a small toy teddy bear last thanksgiving of 1957 which I have most unfortunately lost; and he was a stuffed animal whom I loved and named Blueberry. I liked to bring him with me wherever I'd go.

Mostly, though, we kids hang around the house and play with our friends, the Skolsky kids, in the tanbark area of our backyard when the weather's nice. It's where we have a sandbox, a big log cabin we can play inside of and a cool swing set with a curvy slide that lets us fly down and out onto the soft tanbark.

Our backyard is very private, with a gorgeous croquet lawn and a tall willow hedge running all around the perimeter of the yard, along with a big bunch of splashy lilac bushes arranged in a straight line that separates our tan bark park from the grass and croquet set located just behind our house sunroom and next to our outdoor patio, where our barbecue is located.

Tulips grow there in riotous profusion by the barbecue patio corner. The other side of the sunroom is lousy with those ornery and bossy rose bushes. They are *such petulant* prima donnas, those arrogant roses with their thorny personalities and prickly haughty priggery. Mr. Chips has no patience for them either, especially when they toss their insolent heads in the wind.

The rose bushes *do* smell nice on their side of the sunroom; I'll give them *that;* but they're *such* an annoying pain!

The elegantly aromatic lilacs and tulips around the tan bark and the patio smell just as beautiful on the other side of the sunroom; and unlike the horrid roses, *they* are mostly friendly and breezy.

The croquet set on our backyard lawn behind the sunroom is always ready for play in the late spring and just before summer vacation.

My older brother Alec acts like he's king in the backyard; and that's because he *is*. "Let's play a game of croquet, M!" he says to his friend Morley Skolsky, who whizzes through our backyard, as dashing as Sir Lancelot, in his miniature go-cart.

Sharon, my older sister who's as pretty as a queen of the realm, asks Sadie Skolsky, Morley's younger sister who's visiting for a play date, if she'd like to join a croquet match on the backyard lawn with us boys.

"Why yes I would!" Sadie says mellifluously. She's as beautiful as Guinevere, whom I'm reading about in my paperback books of fairytales, along with my other well-worn books on the land of *Oz*. I carry them about with me in a tiny rucksack on my back.

Mother comes to the opened sliding glass door of the sunroom next to the patio and announces, "Jeffrey, both your schoolteacher and principal are coming over to discuss your disruptive behavior in your grammar school class!" she announces, smiling enigmatically like *The Mona Lisa* because of the sheer ridiculousness of it all.

"Did you want me to be present and accounted for?" I ask her very politely. I'm always extremely deferential with Mother.

"No, I do *not!*" Mother responds, "I'll let them catalog all of your nonexistent personality flaws in the privacy of our sunroom, dear!" she laughs, "though I'm sure you'll hear it all with the sunroom sliders opened on three sides!" she confirms, "so please be very discreet if you're eavesdropping, dear!" she adds as I hear the wheels of a car screech cartoonishly around the corner of Sunset Lane and Elm Ridge before jamming to a stop out front of the house, just like that wicked old Cruella DeVil in the brand new book that's so popular in our school library.

I just *knew it* was *them.* Whenever I see them together in the principal's office, Miss Stinkey and Miss McCracken remind me of the two ladies on the cover of one of Mother's favorite coffee table books that is displayed in our gorgeous living room, where all of her grand canvases of surrealism adorn the walls, like an homage in schadenfreude to the European artistic sensibilities of the interwar years. (Sidebar: I told you I was advanced for my young age.)

The fancy hardcover book I refer to fits in perfectly with Mother's gestalt and is entitled *Gertrude Stein and Alice B. Toklas in Pre-WW-II Paris.* It's an amazing book; and, just as I love Mother's collection of iconoclastic splashy paintings, I adore the brilliant artworks those famous ladies collected much earlier in the twentieth century; as well as the famous personalities and artists they befriended long *long* before either I or my mother were born.

But, unlike Miss Stein and Miss Toklas, whom I *do admire,* I don't like my teacher and her heavy-set gal pal, my school principal, and not because of *what they are,* but because of *whom they've become.*

And even at eight years of age, I can see the difference: — that they are depressingly just a couple of stuck up old cranky antediluvian prigs who don't care a fig about me or my marvelous precocity. That's ok because my intellect and my vocabulary are the bricks and mortar of my castle rock. They are my impenetrable walls, even at eight years of age.

In my family, everyone else is a smarty pants too. My birth father was a doctor as was his dad, not to mention my stepfather, who is also a doctor; and my brother says he'll be one too. Brilliance runs in the family, of course; but I have a better vocabulary than any of them because I read *Webster's Dictionary* for entertainment.

Along with my serious reading, I also enjoy winning at games. And on that score, nothing will stop me from trying to wallop my brother and his friend Morley in croquet today.

****

While we are getting our croquet balls ready for play in the backyard and our teams are being chosen as well, I overhear Miss Stinkey say through the open sliders of the contiguous sunroom, "Jeffrey was talking out of turn during finger painting class recently and this *has got to stop if he's to stay enrolled at North School!*" she bellows in her stentorian voice.

"What *exactly* did he say?" Mother asks demurely, restraining a giggle as I happen to see her shadow through the screen doors of the sunroom, and she is smiling at me on the croquet lawn. While spying on their luncheon meeting, I'm officiously getting ready to play a round of croquet with the gang. You see, I can multitask too. I'm not just erudite and loquacious; but I'm also a bit of a ham and a virtuoso when it comes to braggadocio and showing off, which means I'll have to own a Rolls Corniche someday.

"He was showing off again and telling the kids in class with who!—"

"I think you mean, with *whom*," I hear Mother pedantically correct her.

"*With who, with whom, whatever!*" Miss Stinkey continues exasperatedly; and, like a steamroller, rolls right on over my inelegant charms, rudely saying "anyway, your impossible little boy was finger painting the other day and telling the other kids in class that his favorite artist, Jackson Pollack, paints sort of like him when *he's finger* painting; really, how utterly, absolutely ridiculous!"

"Why's that?" Mother asks simultaneously coquettishly, deferentially, diplomatically and with a subtle note of irony in the lilt of her voice, a nearly impossible mélange of emotions that only a true genius of the art of tête-à-tête could *ever* pull off without a hint of sarcasm.

"Everyone *knows* Mr. Pollack is a no-talent fraud!" the principal says caustically, "after all, he just pours paint on a canvas, something even our children who are finger painting wouldn't *dare do!"*

"Mr. Pollack has passed away. It's not nice to talk ill of the dead!" Mother states succinctly.

"He's dead; how nice!" the principal interrupts.

Ignoring her caustic humor, Mother continues, "his paintings are in the Museum of Modern Art in New York. Maybe the kids should try and emulate him!" Mother says, looking through the porch screens and out at us on the backyard lawn, continuing, "he was an extraordinary artist!" Mother announces confidently. I happen to notice her looking casually around the sunroom and neighboring living room at the big splashy modern art canvases that adorn *all* the walls of the first-floor common areas.

"Your impertinent son brings his little paperbacks of *Grimms Fairytales* and the *Oz* books to school with him, and he shares them with the kids in his class!" Miss Stinkey says, "and that's just ridiculous, for Pete's sake; he's only eight and not all of the other kids his age are reading those more advanced books yet!"

"Well, perhaps they should be; but, yes, I understand ladies. Jeffrey is precocious; and... " she mentions, not skipping a beat while switching subjects to their luncheon served by Carol, the cook, "please have a watercress sandwich and some sarsaparilla, won't you?" Mother offers, as the ladies take China plates, cloth napkins, finger sandwiches from a multi-tiered silver tray and then pour a beverage of the exotic amethyst colored concoction from one of two crystal Waterford decanters, the other being an emerald green.

"Or would you ladies prefer crème de menthe?" she kvells as she looks out at me with my croquet mallet in hand in the yard.

"Crème Demented?" the principal interrupts sarcastically again, not stopping Mother, who then states, "yes, Jeffrey, like my other older children before him, is very precocious and has an encyclopedic vocabulary for a boy his age, I must admit!"

"That's ridiculous too because it makes him too pushy and aggressive in class!" Miss Stinkey says.

"Yes, I know; I see him reading Schopenhauer, Proust and the *Encyclopedia Britannica!*" Mother adds, trying to sound resigned, but just egging on the old witches.

"That's just as ridiculous because no impressionable boy should be reading Schopenhauer or the encyclopedia and certainly not Proust, never *Proust*, that degenerate, for heaven's sake! Thankfully though, I recall your two older children having been a joy at North School, Mrs. Vetch!" The principal, changing the subject, announces loudly, as my brother beams like a king while he's getting ready to practice hitting a croquet ball with his mallet.

"Jeffrey is reading the *Wall Street Journal* and says he wants to be a millionaire at thirty by getting his money to work for *him!*" Mother announces proudly to the ladies, egging them on, "he just loves compound interest!"

"Why that's positively ridiculous; after all, *everyone knows* that you work to get money and not the other way around!"

"Well, here in this house, we're open to different points of view, ladies!"

"Well, that's preposterous and like going through the looking glass to Wonderland, Mrs. Vetch; and I'll have you know that I punished your son Jeffrey the other day by not letting him go to the fire station with our class recently because he was frivolously talking out of turn in our class against my express orders and he was sent directly to the principal's office *yet again!*" Miss Stinkey says haughtily, as the arrogant roses ringing the sunroom out back gavotted in their subtle agreement with the wicked old witch after a brief gust of wind blows out of the west and down toward the ravine, where the bluebells and asters shiver in resplendent silence, not daring to contradict the old biddies and their nasty ditty.

Looking out the sunroom screens toward the woods and shady ravine where hostas grow in magnificent profusion, Mother announces, "I have no objection to you running your school and classes exactly as you see fit, ladies!" a nearly undetectable snicker in her tone that betrays her true perspective while being deferential in not wanting to ruffle any more of their hirsute feathers, as the two old ostriches snort down their food and gulp their drinks.

Mother, to her credit, remains respectful in their presence and in complete agreeable concord with the educational matrons' strict and unpleasant polemic. After all, alienating them would be unwise, even if I disagree with their viewpoint; and, even at eight, I understand the merits of diplomacy, having read about Talleyrand when I was perusing the encyclopedia one day recently.

"My advice is to send him away to prep school as soon as possible, just like your son's idol, Mr. Winston Churchill, you know, who was summarily shipped off at five!" Miss Stinkey announces.

Just then in the backyard as I am eavesdropping on the ladies, Davie Skolsky, Morley's younger brother who looks like a giant egg, Humpty Dumpty, shows up and asks, "can I play too?"

"Yes, of course!" Sharon says, as she gesticulates toward the sunroom and caustically whispers to me, "stop acting like the cowardly lion and screw up the courage to stand your ground with those two old harridans!"

I can see they are getting ready to leave our house after their rant and without even noticing us kids in the backyard having fun during one of the very last late spring weekends.

After their luncheon and tête-à-tête, I can observe Mother walk them out of the sunroom and on into the living room with its big modern art canvases adorning the walls.

"I can see where your youngest son gets his precocious interest in modern art!" I hear the principal say as they are departing.

I am not going to worry about those fussy old ladies at all. And I am determined not to like them one bit either.

But for now, I'll focus on our croquet game and my friends and siblings and how much fun our backyard is in the late spring.

You see, I'm not really a troublemaker at all. I'm just a really young kid who's smart for his age, that's all. Why, when I called Davie the Marquess De L'Oeuf recently because he's so fat and loves eating grilled hotdogs cooked in butter, he was flabbergasted; and he said, 'you mean the marquis of beef, don't you?' and I just dropped the subject!

I love playing games of all kinds in our backyard. It's like a whole make-believe world back there. Mother's arrogant rose bushes are in back too, as is a small stream at the bottom of our ravine in the corner of our backyard and woods, where bluebells and daffodils grow riotously in the summer.

It's very pretty in our backyard and we always have fun playing croquet on our perfectly mowed lawn.

Mr. Chips, Schopenhauer, Snowball and Gopher like to chase each other when they're not chasing our croquet balls or running after Oodles, the neighbor's cat and Johnnie, the friendly auburn-haired neighborhood squirrel.

Why, just yesterday, one of those pernicious pet animals of ours must have purloined Blueberry; and now, I can't find him. Where could my best buddy and little blue bear be? He's as wonderful and rare as a persimmon growing in winter! I must try to find him right after our afternoon croquet game because Blueberry has disappeared!

CHAPTER TWO: BLUEBERRY HAS VANISHED!

Well, let me tell you what happened after our croquet game. I looked all over the house for my little blue bear whom I had named Blueberry, and I couldn't find hide nor hair of him.

"Do you know where he is?" I asked Snowball; and our tiny toy Pomeranian barked, "no I don't know where he is, Master Jeffrey!"

When I went outside, I spied Johnnie, our friendly squirrel, who was climbing up one of the hawthorn trees growing higgledy piggledy down the ravine ridge and across from the small garden of arrogant rose bushes by the house; and after I checked with that rascally critter, he shook his bushy tail back and forth, grinned his toothy smile, signaling 'no, sir' as well, then scampered off into the upper reaches of the autochthonous tree limbs.

As I walked around the corner of our

Georgian style house and past the patch of imperious rose bushes below Mother's bedroom, I saw Schopenhauer, our golden lab, dutifully trailing after his buddy, Mr. Chips, our toy German schnauzer, who was, as usual, irritable, cranky and barking maddeningly at the pale mauve colored tulips, still glittering with traces of pearlescent morning dew and tossing their heads insolently in the breeze in the most ostentatiously taunting fashion, annoying our cutely angry little gray-haired puppy, who was in no particular mood to help me or anyone else find Blueberry.

And finally, of course, there was Oodles, the neighbor's adorable rotund gray American shorthair cat, petulant as usual, clumsily scrambling up one of the bushes between us and our neighbor's yard while chasing a large elegant monarch butterfly that fluttered by her flamboyantly and then teased our miniature schnauzer into a friendly double chase up the tree, caterwauling all the way along the trunk and branches of the hawthorn to where they saw a perfectly gorgeous silent white Persian cat sitting quietly and absolutely motionless in the neighbor's gabled third floor open window like Michelangelo's *Madonna.* Her feline composure was one of calmness, devoid of emotion and simply staring at the frenetics below while slightly shaking her head inscrutably, as if to say to all three of them:— the butterfly, the cat and the schnauzer,— 'what a bunch of drama queens!'

****

The fact was that not one of them would help me locate my favorite lost teddy Blueberry. Then, all of a sudden, as if in a dream, I happened to see Alec's pet rabbit, Gopher, all elegantly attired and dashing out of a small pets' swinging pass-through in the kitchen side door of our house, where he swept by a couple of empty glass milk bottles, knocking them over in a terrible commotion as he scampered by me.

I considered that my eyes must have deceived me as I blinked twice in utter disbelief and consternation, because our little silver haired pet rabbit was all dressed up in the cutest little tartan plaid imaginable while announcing very distinctly, "I'm late for my cookie date with Blueberry!" as he pulled out and looked at his golden breast pocket watch, then dashed past me and scurried through our tan bark play area, hopping through a small opening in the intervening lilac bushes before rushing through the freshly mowed grass and right on past the croquet set, finally disappearing into the strawberry patch and brambles that were lousy with a multitude of raspberries, bluebells and honeysuckles growing in riotous abandon and profusion all along the gentle slope down the ravine to the little stream, where I pursued him, tripping, falling and then rolling down the wooded slope, vainly trying to keep up with him; for he was most certainly in great haste to make his important assignation with my lost teddy.

This was my one and only chance to see if I might find Blueberry, my very own teddy bear, with whom Gopher was serendipitously meeting that very afternoon at their secret location.

Was I imagining this whole thing? Was Blueberry lost or purloined? What evil machinations had taken place by a cruel fate which had deprived me of my prized teddy? And seeing Gopher all dressed up like the white rabbit, I could only wonder if my eyes were playing tricks with me after recently reading *Alice in Wonderland?* Was our lilliputian rabbit Gopher going to be my very own white rabbit, leading me to a fantasy land like Alice's? Or was this all my vivid imagination and just a dream?

As I fell toward the gurgling brook winding through the forest, I finally thought I had caught a glimpse of him once again. I got up and regrouped, having regained my composure, then continued chasing Gopher, who was flying through the riparian bluebells alongside the jade-colored stream which hugged the ravine's bottom; and it was at that moment when I could see that my eyes *had in fact played tricks on me!* Why, *this* rabbit was just a little gray one with no fancy clothes or pocket watch at all; but I chased him just the same, to see *exactly* where he was going, hoping just perhaps, that he'd lead me to my lost teddy, Blueberry.

But I remembered in a flash that I *had seen Gopher coming through our house side door smartly dressed, hadn't I?* I wasn't sure now what or *whom I'd seen. Perhaps my hay fever allergy medication, Contac, was playing tricks with my mind, as it had done before.*

CHAPTER THREE:
THE MYSTERY
IN THE RAVINE

J ust before he ducked into the brambles surrounding the storm drain tunnel at the head of the ravine, I could have sworn I heard Gopher say, once again, "I'm so very late for my coffee cake date with Blueberry!"

My eyes surely were playing tricks on me once more because here he was, once again, fancily dressed to the nines; and I saw him open up and pop the contents of one of two small plasticine packages into his mouth, which I'd noticed earlier when he'd come out of the laundry room side door of our house. Surprisingly, when I ran down the ravine slope to the entrance of the tunnel, I saw that the unopened clear package he'd inadvertently dropped was one of those distinctive individually wrapped and sealed ruby red hard clear candy packets that Mother and her lady friends kept in their living room decorative dishes. Those forbidden candies of various neon colors were *not* for us kids, but strictly for adult guests and company.

'They're Mothers little treats!' she'd say.

Well, I decided then and there that Gopher's loss, wherever he was, was my gain; so, I sat down on one of the ravine's large moldy boulders right by the babbling brook; and then I opened the sealed cherry red candy package, popping its sugary sweetness into my mouth as I looked up through the cave entrance and toward the sunlight filtering through the forest of trees lining the ravine. I watched the pink powderpuff clouds float by in the angel blue sky like a caravan of cotton candy in heaven.

Just then, Gopher startled me by hopping out of the bushes lining the cave's entrance, again announcing, "I'm late, so very late, for my chocolate and tea date with Blueberry!' as he jumped over a large branch stuck in the stream, completely ignoring my presence and officiously speeding right by me and on into the darkened tunnel without even glancing up to see whose silhouette was there. How rude I thought! Well, perhaps I was invisible; and just maybe, this really *was* a dream!

****

Before I knew what trouble I might

encounter, I was throwing caution to the wind and pursuing the silky little persnickety hare into the darkness of the tunnel, where I espied him disappearing in the ebony mist behind some clogged branches and a log; but it was way too dark to see much in the foul stench of the brackish sewer. And, anyway, I was inconveniently gripped by an unmistakable exhaustion after my chase and suddenly recalled the taste of that delicious candy I had hastily consumed without consideration for its ingredients. I should have known better than to ever devour candy whose wrapper said, *'eat me'*, as Alice did in Wonderland.

Too late for such conjecture, I was simply unable to pursue Gopher any further; so, I decided to take a little breather from further speculation on my sorry state and instead reclined on an astonishingly convenient and humongous soft bed of amber leaves next to the gurgling cel-ray-colored waters of the dank odoriferous storm drain. It was there I curled up, enveloped by my cocoon couch of leaves and where the melodious purling waters of the small shimmering stream glinted ruby and emerald, sapphire and diamond upon the obsidian-colored walls of the cave ceiling, highlighting an allegorical frescoed dreamscape whose story I was too young and inexperienced to understand, while the glimmering pearlescent light show serenaded me into a deep dream sleep. And there I lay for a

long while upon the dark mauve velvet leaf bed of
the ebony tunnel.

CHAPTER FOUR: THE FALL

When I awoke at the end of my diapason dream of waves breaking upon a desolate beach in silvered sentences whose staccato rhythms echoed the murmurs of the cave's babbling brook, I looked toward the white halo at the tunnel entrance, where I saw a glint of aquamarine light and what appeared to be an undinal apparition which transmogrified before my sleepy eyes into our little rabbit, Gopher, who was weirdly wearing a completely different outfit then earlier, including a sparklingly bejeweled scarf as he sped out of the tunnel and downstream along the miniature riverbed while calling out, "I'm so very late for my candy cupcake date with Blueberry!"

The tintinnabulation of a heraldic symphony percussion section rang in my ears as I immediately got up and dusted myself off of the luxuriant potpourri-like bed of woven brown velvet leaves I'd rested on; but I noticed that, along with my tinnitus, I had suffered a small bump on the back of my head, as if I'd either fallen, which was unlikely while I was sleeping, or something had fallen upon my head, which was also unlikely; but thankfully, I didn't have a headache in the slightest and the vertiginous decibels in my ears evaporated as quickly as they had mysteriously appeared.

I didn't have time to consider the oddity of that convexity upon my head another moment because I hadn't a second to lose, if I ever wanted to catch up with that elegantly attired and sartorially resplendent rabbit.

I ran to the tunnel entrance to catch up with Gopher, whom I saw speeding along the riverbed at the base of the ravine's hillside with his diamond scarf fluttering behind him and around his neck as he continued stating, "I'm late, so very late for my whip cream sugar cake date with Blueberry!"

When I came out, I was astonished by how different the world appeared to me. It was as if everything was suddenly in vibrant Kodachrome and technicolor after the obfuscation and chiaroscuro grays of the midnight darkened tunnel; and when I looked up and about, I understood how Dorothy must have felt in Oz, because I,— well,— I immediately noticed that the sky was a bright pink, the clouds were glowing orange, the trees were flaming red, the sun was a cheery blue, the stream was a deep rich murky purple and the flowers wore a rainbow of fabulous gems of many colors, and they were waving upon the banks of the rill in the gentle summer zephyrs; but I didn't think anything of it or of the waves of rye undulating in their rhythmic gavotte along the ridge at the ravine's summit because, all I could think of was catching up with Gopher, whom I had witnessed jumping down his rabbit hole at the base of the stream babbling of his tardiness, with his diamond scarf blowing behind him as he disappeared out of sight right next to the storm drain where the purple rivulet poured into it; and, without even thinking, I jumped down the rabbit hole too, mesmerized and in a purple haze, right after him.

I didn't care a fig about his date unless Gopher could reunite me with my beloved Blueberry.

I was falling and falling and falling and falling! As I floated down and down the rabbit hole cave, I passed a giant Christmas tree with ornaments inside of which were scenes of my schoolhouse and my family's backyard and our summer home in the north woods, amongst many other family scenes, as I descended ever lower!

I could see Gopher below me falling too in the dim light of the cave until finally, he simply disappeared in the velveteen darkness; and I finally landed upon a perfectly soft bed of amethyst daffodils and ruby daisies on a velvet emerald mound in a storybook yellow diamond meadow by a little ice cream stream gurgling by a walled and gated yet small gingerbread mansion with candy cane windows, vanilla frosting walls and a chocolate roof next to which there was a butter stick sign post by a path of garnet stones which led into a spooky haunted black forest of cupcake trees and lollypop bushes nearby.

I walked over to read the vanilla chocolate signs showing the way to various places on it. The top sign written in peanut butter boldly announced 'Entering The Land of Excellvania' with a booming voice, the moment I read it; the sign below it pointed right and growled sternly, 'Toward The Haunted Forest, If You Dare!' in a sinister voice; the sign below that pointed left and announced sweetly, 'The County of Candy Land, 5 meters'; the fourth sign on the post pointed in the opposite direction and stated, 'Sapphire City, 7 meters' rather seriously; and the bottom sign announced proudly, 'The Garnet Highway will take you there!' when I stared at it.

How did the moody sign do that? Where I came from, signs didn't speak temperamentally just because you stared at them, as a rule! Such artificial intelligence was foolish! And where exactly was it that the sparkling iridescent road would take me to anyway, I wondered?

CHAPTER FIVE:
CANDY LAND

I marched right on up to the front gate of the little manse, where I read a sign that said *Roselle DeForest*. Well, that's pretty fancy, I thought, as the gate mysteriously opened and I walked right on up the garden path to the magnificent entry door, on which was engraved *Marquess De L'Oeuf on* a small golden plate. The door was made of dark chocolate wood and raspberry sprinkles with a golden chocolate door knocker and lollypop sugar windowpanes. When I went to peel off a couple of raspberry sprinkles to eat, the door knocker slapped my hand and said, "don't do that, monsieur; how'd you like somebody pulling off *your stuffing*?"

"I'm *so* sorry sir! Doors aren't usually so cranky where I come from, sir!" I said somewhat crossly; "and they certainly *don't talk rudely!*"

"Well, they *do here*, in the county of Candy Land and in the great country of Excellvania!" the haughtily imperious front door announced officiously, "and you may call me by my formal moniker, which is Monsieur Le Porte; now, what can I do you for?" The front door said in a somewhat more convivial manner.

"Well, Monsignor!—"

"Monsieur Le Porte!" the petulant door interrupted me, his wooden face turning a bright Maraschino cherry red.

"You certainly look delicious for a plain old door!" I said, speaking uncharacteristically brazenly for a boy my age, "but the fact is that you're made of chocolate and cherry and that's a pretty tasty combina—"

"How dare you speak so salaciously to a personage of my pedigree; really, who do you think you are, Mr. Nabokov, you insolent little troglodyte?"

"It's *whom,* not *who,* when used as a preposition," I corrected that stiff antediluvian pomposity of a door.

"Whatever, don't bother me with your priggery, child!" the dour door admonished me sullenly, "you're as silly as a chocolate teapot!"

Switching subjects so as to avoid any further debate with this embarrassing keeper of the entrance, I demurely asked, "well, *that* sounds delicious; but may I speak to the Lord of the Manor, please, Monsieur Le Porte?"

"You mean, the Marquess De L'Oeuf?" the door asked somewhat more calmly, before adding in a recalcitrant tone of superiority, "he's otherwise engaged!"

"Please kind sir, if you would be so gracious!" I pleaded deferentially, hoping the gatekeeper would have mercy upon me and grant me an audience with his eminence.

The impudent door next announced pompously, "he's enjoying filet of dover sole with fresh asparagus, saffron rice and a slice of persimmon at the moment!"

"I'll just be a moment, kind sir, if you'd permit me the honor of meeting his majesty, the marquis!"

Interrupting me, the difficult door announced, "it's Marquess!" as he surprisingly opened up and I entered a front lobby room that looked like the inside of a gorgeous royal tent from Samarkand. Why, I felt like I'd entered one of the tales of *1001 Arabian Nights,* as I peered through the jade gloom of the tent covered lobby with its floating balloon lights scintillating; and, when I squinted, I could make out a shadowy dining room beyond the lobby where an enormous Venetian Murano rainbow glass chandelier hung suspended from high above an elaborate and enormous gilt edged and coffered ceiling, below which was a Louis XV rococo dining set and chairs at which sat a large shiny cream white egg-shaped man.

He was all alone at the head of the large table and dining on a resplendent feast in dimly twinkling candlelight. Around him was a coterie of many handsomely suited servant men standing at attention against the walls and along the sides of the elaborately festooned capacious room. I should have been intimidated by this grandiosity; but oddly, I wasn't in the slightest.

I was at that moment escorted into the dining room by one of the regally accoutered servant men, who were all dressed like the formidable guards at Buckingham Palace. The enormous round man at the head of the table who looked strangely familiar asked me, "who are you and what *possible* business could *you have* that would require interrupting my meal?" he asked petulantly, as he stuffed a miniature buttered cocktail frankfurter into his mouth.

I thought the giant egg was quite rude; and I couldn't quite place *how* I knew him, but I said, "I'm Jeffrey, and I'm looking for my pet rabbit Gopher and my small teddy bear Blueberry!"

"Well, that's a silky thing to do!" the egg-shaped nobleman announced crossly.

"I think you mean 'silly', not silky, Sir!"

"I mean what I say, young man; and if I say silky, then it's silky!" the gigantic egg stated firmly, as all the servants in the dining room nodded their heads in absolutely silent yet virtuous agreement.

"Yes, Sir! That's right, Sir, it's silky, Sir, of course, your emin—, I mean, your highness!" I said meekly, not wishing to agitate him into becoming *too* hard boiled.

"If I were you, I'd follow the ruby path which I saw the little rabbit traverse just a short while ago after he left us, complaining that he was late for some foolishness with frosting and sprinkles or some such dessert. Go now! You can't miss the ruby path because it's right out front!" the corpulent oval egg-shaped man announced loudly.

"The stones of the path are garnets, not rubies, respectfully, Sir!" I corrected him.

"They're rubies if I say so; and I say so, period!" the autocratic curmudgeonly egg stated unhesitatingly, "now go, leave me in peace to finish my repast; and please go chase after your dreams on your own time, young man, and do not ever wander from or leave the ruby path in the forest!" the old yellowing egg said, a slight crack appearing on his furrowed brow.

"Yes, your honor!" I stated reverentially, as I bowed and quickly departed the place; finding myself back outside and on the sparkling dark red path, which I wandered down until I'd followed it into the deep haunted forest, which was gloomy, dank and spooky, with strange animal cries and mysterious looking gnarled trees whose branches encroached upon the narrowed path in an uncomfortable manner. I had to admit; it was a little scary for an eight-year-old boy, all alone and far away from his home, in a distant land in the midst of a growling gnarly forest with autochthonous tree tendrils that reached out to me and glared menacingly at me with their branches akimbo while their canopies gavotted in the wind. Much as they tried, though, those nasty old trees couldn't envelope me in their untoward embrace because I heeded the marquess' advice and never ventured from the serpentine glimmering deep red path that wound its labyrinthine way through the circuitous mansions of the magical verdant forest.

CHAPTER SIX: FOLLOWING IN GOPHER'S FOOTSTEPS

Deeper and deeper into the impenetrable forest I traversed, following the twists and turns of the shimmering dark red path as it curled through the endless gloom like a nightmarish snake, leaving me to wonder if I was in fact lost in the very heart of a lonely darkness. But then I realized I *couldn't be lost* because there was only one path, and I was on it! Was this all merely a dream, I wondered?

I remembered that I just had to stay on that iridescent path and not wander off into the gnarly woods. I recalled what Mother had told me many times about the dangers of wandering off by myself; and frankly, now I was a little regretful that I hadn't followed her sagacious advice.

I next heard the inauspiciously ominous buzz of giant black Presbyterian moths just overhead and then saw a huge brown bespectacled Episcopal beetle dressed in the uniform of an Oxford Don, quietly reading a magnificently leather-bound illuminated manuscript on the absurdly arcane subject of Antidisestablishmentarianism while he sat cross legged on a gorgeously jagged malachite rock hard by the side of the glimmering garnet path.

A huge ecumenical monarch butterfly fluttered right on by, his razzmatazz all aglow, while alligator lizards uncharacteristically floated unfettered in the stillness of the gloaming, an impossibility that transcended all reason.

Finally, and most absurdly, a large midnight purple squid evidently lost and far from his watery world, slithered along and then into the herbaceous border alongside of the path before disappearing into the dense undergrowth like an ink spot in a nonexistent stream. Such disturbing mirages were the stuff of dreams; but was this a dream and if so, whose nightmares were they and why was I playing a minor role in them, I wondered?

CHAPTER SEVEN:
MEETING OLD
FRIENDS

Just when I thought that the path couldn't get any gloomier, I heard a loud crackling noise and the sound of rushing water as I came to a bend in the dark road which opened up to a sunny meadow, a gurgling brook bordered by eglantine and a miniature castle upon a hill that looked like a replica of Colleen Moore's castle dollhouse!

There was a beautiful picket fence around the estate; and grazing upon the emerald meadow were miniature marzipan horses, white chocolate cows and vanilla cake sheep munching diaphanous grass and cotton candy hay. From my distant perspective, the place looked like a Lilliputian fairytale palace, on the side of which was a perfectly proportioned handsome little man, no bigger than a doll really, sweating profusely with his shirt off and splitting wood on a tiny, cute stump.

I reasoned that, perhaps if I walked closer to the idyllic place, their proportions would be in the proper size relative to my stature. A nice idea, I thought, but on marching up the path, I could see that my theory of relativity was misplaced because here, everything was indeed miniaturized. And once again, the little man looked strangely familiar; but I couldn't quite recall where I'd seen him before. Yet, when he looked up at me, I simply said, "hi, I'm Jeffrey; and I'm looking for my pet rabbit Gopher and my teddy bear Blueberry!"

He said, "hi, Jeffrey; I'm Kenneth, and if you knock on the front door of the castle, my wife, the queen, will let you join her for a cup of tea; and she can tell you all about the pesky rabbit that stopped in a short while ago!"

"Thank you, Kenneth, for your hospitality!" I said politely as I went up to the miniature castle and rang the doorbell, whose melody was *Embraceable You.*

A diminutive beautiful blond servant girl who looked like *Rapunzel* opened the front door and said, "I noticed you were talking to the king; may I help you, Sir?" and I responded in the affirmative, whereupon she said, "won't you come in?" which I did. She looked familiar too, like the others. Was this just a continuation of my dream?

I couldn't believe my eyes! It *really did look like a fairytale castle inside!* For a moment, I thought I was in a scale model of Blenheim Palace or Chatsworth House, it was so elegant! Then, a beautifully dressed miniature lady in a gown fit for a queen descended the staircase looking familiar again; and said, "we get so few visitors here, and I understand you may be looking for someone you've lost!" she mentioned as she continued down the staircase to me and held my hand like a loving mother would; although how she *already knew* of my loss, I hadn't the faintest idea!

"Yes, I lost my pet rabbit Gopher and my teddy Blueberry!" I said, almost crying.

"Here's a hanky!" she said, handing me a gorgeous pale blue silk square; "and you can call me Barbara, if you like! And yes, I saw your pet rabbit who called himself Gopher, not long before you got here; and he's attending the same party as we are down Garnet Lane by the gates to Sapphire City, the capital of Excellvania; and if you like, you can join us as our royal guest!" she said.

"Thank you, Your Highness!" I said, assuming she *must be a queen,* "that would be lovely; and just perhaps I'll catch up with that fascinating rabbit Gopher and he'll lead me to my steady teddy Blueberry!" I exclaimed.

CHAPTER EIGHT: THE PARTY

I t wasn't long before the perfectly formed miniature man named Kenneth came indoors to change for the journey to the party which they were attending. And I didn't have to wait long for the king and queen to return to the living room where I enjoyed a fruity beverage that tasted and looked like *Hawaiian Punch,* along with a *Keebler* chocolate chip cookie, served by a little green elf named Flannery.

I had now witnessed both the diminutive king and queen each descend the magnificent circular staircase like the monarchs they surely were, and I was astonished by the charm and elegance of their mannerisms and their garb.

"You ready?" Her Highness, the little lady and queen, asked me after I'd downed my juice and cookie.

"Yes, Your Highness!" I said, as a perfectly attired groomsman held the front door of the castle open for us to board the small gleaming pumpkin shaped coach awaiting our royal departure with its eight miniature white horses festooned with royal plumage.

Off we glided along the shimmering Garnet Road in our splendid carriage to a surprise party where I hoped I'd find my pet rabbit Gopher and perhaps discover the whereabouts of my precious teddy, Blueberry.

CHAPTER NINE: THE WAY BACK HOME

P ast picture-perfect sparkling farms and beautiful golden shimmering meadows we travelled along the garnet paved path until we came in sight of an aquamarine crystal city of sunshine upon a verdant hill, a heavenly looking miniature domed metropolis with tall glass skyscrapers that sparkled an iridescent blue in the bright light.

As our carriage approached quite near the fair city upon the hill, we traveled along the road where a festival was ongoing near the tall gleaming city walls of lapis lazuli; and I could see it was a medieval fair, with jousting and lawn tennis and all manner of games and delights through which women, men and their children wandered, dressed in the clothes of their ancient medieval era.

I saw Robin Hood and King Arthur, Guinevere and Sir Lancelot too; and their visages were, each and every one, so *very* familiar! Why couldn't I recollect how I recognized them? Those famous personages and many others unknown to me were there, mingling with the crowd which bustled about the spacious park in front of the shiny ultramarine city walls.

When our jewel encrusted carriage finally stopped in front of a joyous party sitting at a long turquoise table with an unforgettable personage at its head and holding court by the side of the fair, I was astonished to see him along with many of my old friends from back home and new ones from Excellvania too!

Why, there was Oodles the cat, dressed to the nines as a cool hep hipster feline; and he was chatting it up with Baxter, my mother's black toy poodle, who was elegantly dressed in a stunning Schiaparelli pantsuit and looking like he was all set for a stroll in the Bois De Boulogne with his elegant, diamond encrusted walking stick; and of course Mr. Chips was sartorially clad in a black tuxedo and sporting shiny black leather Ferragamos upon his paws.

"We certainly weren't expecting to see *you* here today!" Oodles meowed, as Baxter and Mr. Chips silently agreed, "this was one person that we'd *never have* thought would show up in *this* setting; but it's nice to see you, just the same, boss!" Oodles purred to me.

"You mean this is a dream?" I asked Mr. Chips.

"Only if you believe it is, silly!" Johnnie, the crafty clever neighborhood squirrel piped up as Mr. Chips grinned. Johnnie was an absolute knockout, dazzlingly donned just like the incorrigible criminal Mackie Messer, better known as *Mack the Knife,* although why, I couldn't possibly fathom.

"Why are you decked out like that small-time hood, *Mack the Knife,* with your chinos and large pewter belt buckle, unbuttoned faded gray shirt and navy beret?" I asked Johnnie.

"Hey, don't ask me, kid, it's your dream, after all!" Johnnie chirped.

"I don't think so, Johnnie; I'd *know* if this was my dream; and I don't *ever* dream of *Oz* or *Wonderland, either;* no, not *ever!*" I announced.

Finally, I saw *him,* the giant egg of a man I'd met way back on the other side of the haunted forest. And there he was, sitting in the place of honor at the head of the table, just as I'd expect a man of his eminence would, the saturnine Marquess De L'Oeuf, looking radiant, surrounded as he was by his entourage of handsomely outfitted manservants.

"Come, sit over by me at once!" the Marquess insisted of me; but I demurred politely.

"His Highness, the King, as well as the Queen, have both graciously included me at their end of the table; but thank you for your kind offer, Your Excellency!" I said, not wanting to burn any bridges in the fair land of Excellvania, especially with this esteemed personage, in case I required his help in returning to my hometown, Glencoe, in the American heartland.

The biggest surprise of all at the party was finally catching a glimpse of the creature I'd been pursuing all along: — my little Gopher, our pet rabbit, whom I was startled to see wearing an artist's bohemian outfit and looking every bit like Picasso in Paris pre-WWII.

"I was hoping you'd lead me to the teddy I'd lost; and I'd finally be reunited with Blueberry once again!" I announced rather seriously to Gopher, who looked over to the King's entourage and then just silently smiled, as if he knew a gem of a secret whose sparkle he wasn't revealing.

And that was *that,* as they say, because, in that split second, I could at last see that, having appeared out of nowhere, my long-lost prize teddy was clearly now an august member of King Kenneth's court and retinue. As I watched Blueberry dutifully follow in the King's footsteps and sit next to him, I was beginning to understand what that meant for our friendship.

At seven years of age, I had been gifted him,

yet I hadn't planned on losing Blueberry at eight; but I *had to let my teddy go,* especially if he wished to stay in the charming county of Candy Land in the great country of Excellvania. I had no right to imprison him outside of my dream. I couldn't be *that* selfish.

What a real scene stealer my teddy Blueberry was that day! He was dressed in a shimmering dark blue Brooks Brothers suit with a pink ascot around his neck.

"Jeff!" Blueberry said to me privately as he handed me the matching pink sash he had in his breast pocket, "I know how much you love me, and here's a memento to remember me by forever; and I thank you for all you've done for me!—"

"I don't really think I've done *anything special,* Blue—!" I interrupted him.

"But I just want you to know I'm staying here in Excellvania; and I won't be returning with you to the Midwest," Blueberry continued, interrupting me, "I hope you understand that I'm needed here; but you'll always have me in your thoughts, I know that!" he concluded.

"I don't think I'll ever forget you or find a teddy as cute as you, Blue," I said, somewhat dejectedly.

"I think you will, just you wait!" Blueberry told me, sounding just as confident as you'd expect a perfectly blue teddy bear ought to be.

Well, I thought to myself, I'd just have to wait and see about that; and in the meantime, I'd just enjoy the Sapphire City party at the Candy Land County fair in the beautiful country of Excellvania.

****

I could see that everyone was having a fine time at the fair. It was a party fit for a king and a queen; and when I, along with the royal couple, Kenneth and Barbara, joined them all at their festive gathering, I felt like I knew them all, even the new friends I'd just met in Excellvania; but I didn't know *why* that I felt I knew them. Yet in a dream state, you can *know* someone or something with an assurance that is the very stuff of dreams!

"I'll let the Marquess tell you what we're celebrating at the party here at the Sapphire City Fair!" Queen Barbara whispered in my ear, as Guinevere came over, curtsied and kissed her on both cheeks.

After King Arthur and Sir Lancelot joined us, along with all the Knights of the Round Table standing guard along with the Marquess's regally groomed male servants, a line of magnificently dressed courtiers raised their horns simultaneously, their clarion call echoing throughout the fairgrounds and silencing the crowd.

Then, the fat, egg shaped Marquess said, "welcome all to our fair land of Excellvania and our charming city, Sapphire, where we promote harmony and goodwill for all.

"Today is a special day, because I have appointed Lord Blueberry, our beloved bear, as the new Lord Mayor of Sapphire, our shining metropolis in the very heart of the county of Candy Land. And it is he whom I trust will manage our fair shining city well in my absence and until my return," he said, adding "if ever!" in an aside which he whispered to me, before continuing with bravado, "I have official business in the metropolis of Glencoe in the state of Illinois and in the great heartland of America, far beyond the stratosphere of clouds; and the business that I must conduct requires that I take Sir Jeffrey," the Marquess said, nodding toward me to bow, which I dutifully did, then pulling me very close to him as he continued, "it is he whom I have appointed my Special Counsel to help guide me on my journey back to the American Midwest, where I hale from and where I will consort with the many fine leaders of that great heartland which that esteemed nation of America is famous for!

"Please take care to honor and respect your

King Kenneth and Queen Barbara of our fair land of Excellvania as well as your new Lord Mayor Blueberry of the great city of Sapphire in the county of Candy Land; and know that I will return as soon as Jeffrey and I conclude our business back at my old homeland of America and great state of Illinois," the Marquess stated to the throng confidently, winking at me as if to privately convey that his return was in serious doubt.

"Really, we're returning to Illinois, my home state too?" I asked, whispering to him.

"Yes!" the Marquess responded quietly in an aside to me, continuing loudly to the assembled throng, "please know you are all in good hands here and I will return soon!" the Marquess said, holding tightly onto me as he unexpectedly began to lift off the ground of the fair in the heat of the day, with me the size of a mere windup toy in his great eggy arms.

The crowd at the fair rushed to bring us back to the ground; but we two floated up into the sky too quickly as he grabbed my hand tightly in his. I had vainly reached out to Blueberry to join us, but to no avail.

"Please don't let Blueberry stay behind!" I said to the Marquess, as we two floated ever higher in the rainbow sky.

"I am staying right here taking care of

this fair city and it's wonderful people, Jeffrey!" Blueberry called out to me, "but you'll always have me in your memory back in Glencoe, so take care forever!"

"He must stay behind in your memory!" the Marquess said to me as we floated ever higher, "Blueberry will help guide the great Sapphire City and tend to all those fine denizens of that fair burg there, as well as all those partygoers now at the fair in the fair land of your fairytale memories!" the Marquess said repetitiously, as we floated through the cumulus clouds and on up into the scintillating stratosphere, where we were carried on the diaphanous wings of cherubic angels all the way back in space and dream time to the prosaically normal life I remembered so well, a life that I never appreciated as a boy of seven half as much as the more mature boy of eight I had become. *That* was Blueberry's effect on me, instilling within me a sense of belonging and of kinship that was precious.

After the colorful fantasylands I'd just visited, the normality of the great American Midwest appeared black and white by comparison; but beautiful and familiar, nonetheless, and wonderfully comfortable. Ah, Glencoe; how lovely its memory has always been!

CHAPTER
TEN: LOST!

"What about my teddy Blueberry? Is he lost forever?" I asked the Marquess, as the giant egg of a man holding my hand floated to earth along the sandy shore of the Glencoe beach at Park Avenue, very early on a warm summer Sunday morning when no one was around and everyone in the little village was still fast asleep in dreamland.

"Just remember Blueberry fondly as the teddy you once had, and you'll never forget him!" the Marquess said to me.

"Yes sir," I respectfully answered him glumly, a note of resignation in my tremulous voice.

"The perfection of his memory will always be with you!" the giant egg said, as we landed on a rock on the beach which punctured his shell and caused the air inside of him to quickly dissipate as he shrunk to the size of a normal sized egg, which I just as quickly put in my pocket, along with Blueberry's pink sash he'd given me as a remembrance and present I'd always cherish.

CHAPTER ELEVEN: WAKING UP!

J ust then I was jarred by the sight of Cruella DeVil's huge black limousine, which came charging down the concourse traversing the Glencoe cliffs and alongside of the concrete staircase which led to the beach.

I was walking up the stairs with the little egg in my pocket and on my way to return home, a little sad without my best buddy and teddy, Blueberry, when I saw Miss DeVil standing at the side of her huge gaudy Isotta Fraschini automobile, looking as demonic as Norma Desmond in the cinema classic, *Sunset Boulevard*.

"Get into this car at once!" Madame DeVil commanded, "you're too young to be wondering around the Glencoe beachfront alone in the morning!"

"I think you mean wandering, not wondering, Miss DeVil!" I announced humorously.

"How dare you correct me!" she announced

imperiously as she pulled at my sleeve to get into her exotic Italian limousine.

"I don't get into stranger's cars, and no one is stranger than you!" I announced firmly, as Madame DeVil continued to yank at my sleeves.

"You'll do as I say!" Madame DeVil ordered; "and anyway, you don't know a thing about me because I'm a brand-new character in your dream!" she announced agitatedly.

"You're not brand new, Miss DeVil; and, no, you can't make me, no you can't!" I said, "and I do know about you because our librarian Miss Cottle has been reading us the brand-new book, 101 Dalmatians, which you're in, Miss DeVil!" I said, as I suddenly awakened, shuddering from my dream.

I was no longer at the Glencoe Beach. No, I was back home in my very own bedroom, where I saw my brother Alec and my sister Sharon and my mother and my stepfather Adolph and the milkman and even some of my friends, all reminding me of the characters I'd met in my dreamland.

"How long was I out this time?" I asked my stepfather, remembering the time I'd fainted earlier in the spring.

"Nearly a week this time; and, boy, you sure had quite a bump on your head from your fall in the storm drain, and we weren't sure you'd!—" my

111

stepfather said, choking up.

"But you were all there in my dream, all of you, even our pets and my teddy too!" I said as everyone comforted me and each other in a knowing look of silent camaraderie and gentle kindness.

"We're all glad you're back with us!" Paul and Carol, Mother's devoted chauffeur and cook, said simultaneously.

"You remember it all?" Alec asked.

"You were all in my dream!" I said, pulling the cracked hard-boiled egg out of my pajama pants pockets as I looked around my bedroom, "you and you and you and you, too!" I said happily, as I saw Sadie and Morley Skolsky and my brother Alec and my darling precious sister Sharon and of course my mother Dolores and stepfather Adolph.

Arrayed on my bed were all our pets; and at the open bedroom window were my kindergarten teacher Miss Stinkey and the grammar school principal Miss McCracken, who were quietly smiling in unison. "But how did this egg get in my pocket?" I asked the milkman, who winked at me.

"Don't ask me!" he said, "I just deliver 'em, son!" he laughed.

"Oh, I remember now how that egg got in my pocket. I floated back to earth from faraway in the county of Candy Land with the help of the Marquess De L'Oeuf, a giant egg of a fat guy, who blew up to the size of a gigantic balloon, like the one which the Wizard of Oz flew back to Kansas in with Dorothy!" I said, as everyone in the room smiled gently and laughed just a little bit with a smidgen of redness in their eyes.

"I see you've been reading your Oz books; how nice!" said my stepfather, his voice cracking a little as he looked at the stack of famous children's books on my nightstand next to my bed.

"Well, you have to tell us who of us were in your dream, Jeffie!" Sadie Skolsky whispered cutely, as Mr. Chips grabbed the egg out of my hand and swallowed it whole.

"You were there dressed as Guinevere and your older brother Morley was dressed as Lancelot and your younger brother Davie was the giant egg who brought me back home by floating up into the sky over Excellvania like a balloon!" I said.

"Mr. Chips just ate the egg!" Sadie said.

"It's only a regular egg now silly" I said.

"Well, that's pretty fanciful!" Alec mentioned.

"Yes, and you were King, Alec; and Sharon was queen of the realm!" I said.

"Aww, that's sweet!" Sharon responded

adorably.

"And Oodles and Baxter were there too, courtiers to the monarch and all dressed up like a cool cat and hip pooch should be!" I said.

"Jeff, we hope you feel better soon!" Miss Stinkey said from the open window, as she and her driver Miss McCraken waved goodbye, then departed, after which we could hear their pale green '54 Plymouth peal out of the driveway demonically with Miss McCracken at the wheel.

"Miss Stinkey was Cruella DeVil and Miss McCracken was one of her henchmen in my dream," I announced, whispering, as I vividly remembered that my kindergarten teacher and our grammar school principal had conspired to cruelly keep me from visiting the fire station in the village with my class because I'd been talking out of turn during a lesson, and that nightmare was no dream.

"But you were all there and now I'm home and even though I lost my teddy Blueberry and he's never coming back; I still have you all!" I said, as Gopher, our little rabbit, wagged his tail at the windowsill and knocked over a brown package resting there which someone must have placed strategically for just such a serendipitous discovery; but who?

Opening it up after Sharon had handed it to

me, I was thrilled to see a perfectly tan teddy bear, every bit as cute as Blueberry, and an exact twin except for his light brown color.

"I'll never forget Blueberry as long as I live; but Joshua, my new brown teddy, is perfectly perfect!" I said, instantly naming him. "Whom do I thank?" I asked Sharon.

"No one!" she demurred. "It's a mystery!" Sharon said, with a nod and a wink, like she knew the truth, but wasn't telling me.

"You're perfectly perfect too, just as you are, dear darling sister and just like my new teddy, Joshua Tree!" I said, giving him a full and proper name and thanking my sister, just the same.

CHAPTER TWELVE: THERE'S NO PLACE LIKE HOME!

And of course, looking back on my little child's tale, twice told now after all these many years and embellished a bit, of course it was all true, every word of it, just as I'd written so very *very* long ago in my little diary as a boy of eight; a story which I've now shared here with only you, along with a few of my later annotations. My Lilliputian story in my cute little kid's handwriting in my toy diary about a place faraway I dreamed of called Excellvania and a county of Candy Land where I met a cast of characters as well as a giant egg, is all the stuff of one little kid's vivid imagination and nothing more.

If its confectionery effect lasts for just a moment and dissolves as quickly as candy, I'm ok with that because I can *still* fondly remember the tale of my first teddy Blueberry. And the recollections I have of my brother Alec and sister Sharon when I was just a kid in 1958, I still hold near and dear to my heart, all these years later. I will always be grateful to them for the good times I recall in glowing detail, memories as bright as the soft orange sunset over Bluff Street in Glencoe on a warm hazy summer evening.

And though I'm no longer that kid anymore; and haven't been for many *many years,* when I think back to long *long ago* and all those good times we shared at our Glencoe home back then in the late 1950's, I am imbued with the glowing comfort of a time before I knew anything about *anything at all really,* when I fell down a hole chasing our rabbit, Gopher, and dreamed a dream of self-discovery in search of my unforgettable teddy bear, Blueberry, whose pink sash still wraps around my desk lamp base in my La Jolla library all these years later, reminding me that I still have my wonderful remembrance of a time, long ago, of my childhood and my cherished teddy!

****

Thank you for letting me share with you this modest little story originally written by me as a kid.

As to the mystery of who gave me Joshua,

the brown teddy, it wasn't resolved until recently, when my sister Sharon dropped by my La Jolla house; and, seeing that pink sash still tied around the base of the library lamp on my desk, asked me, "Jeffrey, were you ever as happy with Joshua Tree as you were with Blueberry and his pink sash all those many years ago?" and I smiled at her and said, "darling, I never told you that pink sash was Blueberry's; but thank you for the gift of Joshua all those years ago, you really are so special!"

And, you know what? With a wink and a smile once again and a friendly nod in silence, Sharon finally told me *without saying a word* all I needed to know about Joshua and who gave the little brown teddy to me, at long last; and to her, all I can say is, "thank you, darling, always, for being the most perfectly perfect sister a boy could ever imagine!"

And to *you*,— yes, *you!*— who've been reading my little tale of a special little boy and his friends and pets, may I simply say, 'good night and may all of your dreams come true too!'

BOOK III: ME AND MISTER CHIPS

CHAPTER ONE: NEW YEARS DAY 1959 WITH ME AND MR. CHIPS

New Years Day 1959

Mr. Chips is my tiny snowball sized ten-month-old German schnauzer puppy. He will grow to be the size of a football within a year. He's very cute and always ornery. His hair and tiny tail are closely cropped and gray. He may look old but he's just a baby; and he's *always* barking, like *always!* And I am the *only* person who understands what he is saying, because a kid knows his puppy better than *anyone, right?*

My name is Jeff and I'm nine years old. I have a little gray hair too, which my doctor says is very *very* rare for a boy my age and that makes me very special. Funny, but I don't *feel* old *at all. But I'm very precocious* because I read a lot for a kid my age. I'm always perusing the *Wall Street Journal, The New York Times, The Encyclopedia Britannica and Webster's Dictionary* for new ideas, new ways of thinking and new words.

Why, just last year, Mother helped me open up a passbook savings account at the Glencoe National Bank with my allowance money, and I was fascinated by the accrued interest that was credited to my account each and every month. When my funds reach a level high enough, I'll buy a share of IBM in addition to the odd lot Mother has given me already. At nine, I know I'm a capitalist. I want my capital to work for me someday so that I can spend my time writing. That's because I want to be a writer.

In the meantime, Mr. Chips is my constant companion; and he and I have been inseparable since the day Mother and Alec brought him home.

Why, just last week, when I went downstairs early, I found that Mr. Chips had snuck out of our bedroom in the middle of the night and was nestled comfortably amongst the presents under the Christmas tree and wearing a pretty red bow tied around his neck while barking incessantly! Mother said that Santa must have brought the bow just for him. Thank you, Santa, for dressing him up and making my dreams of a cute little querulous barking puppy underneath the Christmas tree come true!

Mr. Chips is always cross and cranky; but never scary because he's so tiny he can fit in the palm of my hand!

Mr. Chips and I live a sweet life in Glencoe with my unique family, including my demanding but generous mother, Dolores; my autocratic and challenging stepfather, Adolph; my haughty and protective older brother Alec and my prima donna and charming older sister Sharon, who's a hoot! They're almost *never at home!* That's because they're *always* very busy elsewhere with adult stuff.

Mother and Adolph spend a lot of time at the country club; and my brother and sister are *always* off somewhere doing big kid stuff with their friends.

Alec rides go-carts with his friend Morley while my sister and her friends enjoy their sophisticated dollhouses, cute Barbie dolls and fashionable China tea sets.

That leaves plenty of time for Mr. Chips and I to be by ourselves, which is just the way we like it, because we're best friends forever, me and my puppy. We both enjoy my neighborhood in Glencoe, including our streets on Elm Ridge Drive and Skokie Ridge, both situated in between Dundee Road to the South, Greenbay Road to the north, Vernon Road to the east and Hohlfelder Road to the west, especially at Halloween, when we go neighborhood trick-or-treating, and our part of town feels much larger in the spooky darkness.

But today is the *most* special one of the year because it is New Years Day of 1959 and Mr. Chips and I are celebrating by making a big snowman with my older brother Alec.

Alec is the best older brother in the *whole* world because he's always looking out for me when he isn't pretending to be a bully; but I don't mind one bit. Alec looks like Wally on *Leave It to Beaver,* and he and his friend Morley are popular with the girls in their school class, like *very* popular, if you know what I mean. The girls in their class are always fawning all over Alec and Morley, as pretty girls do over handsome boys; yech, and what a pain!

****

I look at my *Dick Tracy* watch and realize it is past time for me to make my New Year's resolutions. I ditch that plan and instead decide to get ready to build that New Year's Day snowman with Alec.

"Let's go!" Mr. Chips barks, as he prances out of Carol and Paul's room at the end of the kids' bedroom wing and several symbolic stair steps down from us. Carol's the maid and cook; and Paul, the chauffeur and houseman. They're married and are very helpful to Mother and us all. Why, just earlier today, they helped Mr. Chips don his miniature fur trimmed parka and Wellington booties for our adventure outside; and Mr. Chips is raring to go!

He is so cute in his little winter outfit that I simply have to tease him and pinch him on his back close to his mini tail! He snarls irreverently, twirls his head and growls at me. He's cute when he playfully snaps. He's just not that scary because he's about as big as a minute or maybe a snowball, *really*.

And, boy, is it snowing *really hard* when we go into the front yard to build our snowman. Mr. Chips, who is so cute in his tiny Scottish plaid parka and his wellies, proceeds to dig up a pile of snow while he barks, "you guys can do this!" which of course is *exactly* what we do!

We build our snowman, with scraggly twiggy hands, bright red cherry tomato buttons, a carrot nose, marble eyes, charcoal teeth and an old beaten up crumpled black and tan straw hat; and when we finish, we dub our snowman Mr. Buttz.

****

With the snowman complete, Alec looks with pride at Mr. Buttz; and then, Alec, Mr. Chips and I walk over to the corner of Sunset Lane and Bluff, where there is a streetlamp out of view of our house; and, with Mr. Chips barking loudly while digging up piles of snow and egging us on, Alec and I throw snowballs high up at the glass panes of the streetlamp in order to knock them out.

What scalawags we three are, what audacious miscreants! Mr. Chips is our cheerleader and Alec nails a few of the glass panes. The hexagonal panes Alec hits with bullseye accuracy. They shatter after careening to the ground and crashing onto the snowy sidewalk; but my aim is so wonky that I miss the mark by a country mile due to my small size and the sheer height of the tall streetlamp.

The iconoclastic Mr. Chips continues egging us on by barking so loudly that a police car driving by stops to see what all the commotion is about. It's amazing how loud such an itty-bitty puppy can be; but, despite his diminutive toy-like size, Mr. Chips takes the cake for being the loudest thing outdoors in our neighborhood that afternoon, other than the exploding panes of glass that smash upon the ground around us like little bombs!

When the officer exits from his black and

white police vehicle, all a-sparkle with pretty red, white and blue flashing lights, I recognize him immediately from school on the special day that past fall when he came to our class to escort us to the village town hall building for a visit. All the kids in my class got to go to the police and fire station but me because our teacher, Miss Stinkey, sent me to the principal's office for rudely talking out of turn in class.

"Hi, Officer Krupke!" I say innocently as Mr. Chips barks and Alec looks quietly sheepish and apologetic.

"What are you boys doing here?" Officer Krupke asks us as he looks at the broken glass around us and the streetlamp high above, damaged and denuded of its precious beveled panes of glass.

"Throwing snowballs!" I say forthrightly and proudly as Mr. Chips keeps barking at the officer.

"You boys know not to throw snowballs at the streetlamp!" he says, trying to sound like he was scolding us as he looks seriously at the broken panes of glass in the snow which litter the corner of Bluff Road and Sunset Lane, while Mr. Chips continues barking infernally.

"Into the car, you ragamuffin!" the officer orders Mr. Chips, who blithely jumps into the opened car door like a proud lawbreaker!

It could have been a scene straight from a Norman Rockwell cover for *The Saturday Evening Post;* and at nine years old, *even I knew that!* After all, we got *The Saturday Evening Post* and I read it cover to cover every week too!

"Let's get you three home right now!" Officer Krupke says, trying to sound both authoritative and angered, but not doing a very effective job at either; as Alec and I join the unruly Mr. Chips in the back of the police car and then drive off with the lights flashing, the siren screaming and Mr. Chips incessantly barking. I sense that the officer wants to scare us into submission as we barrel around the block like we were in a cartoon, finally pulling into the steep driveway of our Hemphill designed Georgian brick mansion at the pinnacle of our ridge.

Just as the policeman arrives at our garage with his vehicle lights flashing and noisy siren blaring, an aghast looking Mother along with our stepfather Adolph both come running out of the house; and seeing us in back, Mother, peering inside at the metal cage separating us from the front seat and the policeman, hurriedly asks in a deferential tone, "officer, sir, what *on earth* has happened that has caused my boys and their puppy to be in your vehicle?"

"They were throwing snowballs at the

streetlamp!" the officer says matter-of-factly, while Mr. Chips barks vociferously, and we politely wait for the officer's instructions.

"You boys may exit the vehicle at once!" Officer Krupke says, as we pile out of the vehicle and stand at attention for our severe punishment. "But the recalcitrant puppy stays!" the officer says, as he turns to Mr. Chips and announces, "you miscreant, *you* egged them on, *didn't you? You* aided and abetted the criminal behavior of the boys in their property damage, didn't you?" the officer says, as Mr. Chips barks proudly in agreement. "You three confederates must never do this again, you understand?" the officer asks, as Mr. Chips once again barks loudly in agreement.

"Did they break any panes of glass?" Adolph asks the officer politely.

"I'll let the boys answer!" Officer Krupke said.

"I broke three!" Alec said resignedly, a slight note of pride in his voice.

"You'll pay the police department back every penny you owe from your newspaper route earnings," Adolph states bluntly.

"Yes, sir," Alec responds glumly.

"And you?" Mother asks, looking over at me and back at Mr. Chips in the police car.

After Mr. Chips let out a single bark of guilt in the affirmative, I announce, "I tried, but I couldn't throw that high!" I admit, as the officer looks over at our parents, who held back the slightest of smiles at the edge of their lips while the officer's eyes redden momentarily.

"Why does the officer look like he's gonna cry?" I ask Mother.

"He must have gotten a snowflake in his eye, my dear!" Mother says.

"That's right, I *did!*" the officer adds.

"Oh, ok!" I answer, missing the point.

"If you boys promise to never *ever* do that again, to never *ever* break the streetlights, I won't haul you into the police station for your mug shots and fingerprints! And Mr. Chips, if you no longer are an accomplice with the boys in such chicanery, then you too are dismissed and are free to go!" Officer Krupke says in a mock serious voice meant to scare us all as he smiles at Mother and Adolph benignly.

Mr. Chips barks once more in the affirmative, pops out of the back of the police car with his tail wagging and then prances proudly into the back of the garage and over to his puppy bed while Mother and Adolph wish the officer a wonderful New Year. Mr. Chips continues wagging his little tail as he sits in the old puppy bed and quietly barks. I alone hear him bark to us all, "Happy New Year!" as the officer says goodbye, gets in his now silent squad car and summarily backs down our driveway and down Elm Ridge toward Dundee Road.

We go into the house through the garage, close the garage door and then we come through the side entrance to our little library, making sure to leave the back door to the garage open so that Mr. Chips can come in when he has had a chance to nap and compose himself after our difficult afternoon ordeal.

My older sister Sharon, who has come downstairs by now, asks, "what was the police car doing in our driveway?" and in her presence and those of Mother and Adolph as well, Alec and I promise to never throw snowballs at any streetlamp again, as Sharon smiles in silent agreement.

I simply adore Sharon. What a class act of a big sister she is for a younger brother still growing up!

Mr. Chips trots in from the garage, barks in the affirmative and curls up next to the couch as we all get ready to watch the evening news with Huntley and Brinkley on our RCA black and white television.

During the news broadcast as I thumb

through the latest *Saturday Evening Post* after studying Mr. Rockwell's front cover illustration, it occurs to me to try and locate the most prominent gallery which represents the famous artist and send a note there to his attention simply describing the scene earlier in the day at the street corner with the policeman disciplining Alec, me and Mr. Chips as the snowballs and broken panes lay beneath the flickering and damaged streetlamp.

Mother waits for a commercial break in the news broadcast; and then she gets up from her favorite damask covered side chair and closes the back library door leading to the garage.

If a passerby had happened to be walking by and looked through the snow flurries and frosted panes of our library windows facing the driveway and the front yard, we could be seen all gathered together warm and snug on the comfortable couch as Mother returns to her plush side chair and Adolph sits at his desk, glancing at the mail while sipping a scotch on the rocks with a lemon twist, a nightly ritual before dinner in our charming little family room.

Mr. Chips has had a *very long* day. He yawns, let's out one more weak bark, saying, "Happy New Year!" in his own special 'barkalucious' way and falls immediately asleep to Chet Huntley's soothing voice.

CHAPTER TWO: FEBRUARY 14 AND VALENTINE'S DAY WITH MR. CHIPS

By Valentine's Day, I discover one of the prominent galleries representing Mr. Rockwell's work; and I plan on mailing the gallery the letter I've crafted to the famous artist's attention in which I briefly describe the past New Year's scene when we were caught in the act by the officer after we had thrown a few snowballs at our corner streetlamp and knocked out some of its glass panes. After I drop the letter to Mr. Rockwell in the mailbox at the corner, I then put the whole thing completely out of my mind and forget all about it.

****

I have more important stuff to consider this day; after all, it is *Valentine's Day!* Mr. Chips usually accompanies me every school day to North School, but *this* particular Valentine's Day is *extra* special! This day, he is carrying all my valentine cards for my friends in my grammar school in his very own itty-bitty knapsack which is strapped around his back. He looks cute and debonair, my little puppy!

When we arrive at the Vernon Avenue underpass at Greenbay Road, he scampers ahead of me as I park my bike in the miniature triangular pocket park located at the intersection along the south side of the busy commercial thoroughfare.

"Come on, Jeff!" I hear him bark as I run after him.

He dashes ahead of me and through the dark underpass beneath Green Bay Road and on up to the steps leading to the front lawns of North School, after which Mr. Chips next heads over to the opened east side door of the school located close to the teacher's parking lot and roundabout.

By the time I follow him into our classroom, Mr. Chips is alone near the bookshelves, from the lower level of which I could tell he's apparently pulled out a hardcover and is squealing delightfully while perusing the classic beginner reader, *Fun with Dick and Jane* while casually munching on a baby carrot from his knapsack.

He is sitting quietly next to the shattered cobalt-colored remnants of the teacher's favorite deep blue vase which she had won at Riverview Amusement Park and has proudly displayed on one of our classroom's mid-level built-in bookshelves for many years. I know that she has adored and coveted that sentimental vase way more than its token intrinsic value.

As my classmates begin trickling into class, followed by Miss Sea, our inestimable instructor, Mr. Chips, the little iconoclastic sneak, quietly scampers out leaving the bitten off greenery at the top of his carrot next to one of the deep blue shards of broken glass as the only clue to his earlier appearance; but that trace of evidence doesn't implicate him sufficiently.

Miss Sea is *not* in a good mood, and she demands to know who *exactly* it is in our home room who has broken her prized trophy, — her sapphire-colored glass vase! — from Riverview Amusement Park, no less!

I had earlier scowled at Mr. Chips before he disappeared, but before he skedaddled, I had taken the valentine cards from his knapsack as he was getting ready to take off for rosier pastures.

I then hand my teacher her special card with a look of regret and contrition on my face. As my classmates continue to stream in for our Valentine party, I hear Mr. Chips scamper down the main hallway of the school, his paw nails clattering upon the shiny linoleum floor as he lets out a trademark bark before he flies up the central library steps by the administration offices. And by the time I have the opportunity to excuse myself and follow the little vixen up to the second-floor library room in order to escort him out of school for good, he has already grabbed a well-worn edition of *The Little Engine That Could;* and I notice he is giggling and thoroughly enjoying the drawings and softly barking in his silly laughter. I can tell he wants some private time perusing his beloved book when I watch Mr. Chips next saunter through the open second floor stairwell door to the school's spooky attic hallway which runs the length of the eastern side of the building; and in the dim light of the naked overhead lightbulb, I leave Mr. Chips, unafraid of being alone in the endless dark attic while quietly giggling as he paws through the well-worn pages and drawings of the famous book.

I return to the Valentine's party on my own to be with my school friends. I can tell that Mr. Chips just wants to be by himself after breaking the precious blue vase of Miss Sea. I leave him pretending to lick the wounds of his injured ego; while I do my level best to placate sorrowful Miss Sea's sense of loss by taking the blame for Mr. Chips after my clumsy puppy shattered her classic blue glass vase.

"Jeffrey, I know you didn't do it, dear!" Miss Sea says gently.

"You do?" I ask, sounding contrite, nonetheless.

"It was the wind coming in through our windows; and you can see them opened dear, because a bunch of papers on my desk blew onto the floor, as well," she responds resignedly; and prudence being the better part of valor, I conclude that edifying her at this point would serve no one's interest and I remain silently respectful of her and grateful for the serendipitous good fortune of a beneficent fate.

I also know that my heartfelt private regret along with a lovely luncheon for Miss Sea at the house with Mother as hostess which I'll help arrange soon, will hopefully do the trick in helping Miss Sea feel better, along with keeping Mr. Chips from barking in her presence and disturbing her delicate neurasthenic fragility, an arduous task which is almost always a near impossibility given Mr. Chips' cacophony.

When I go to collect him in the school attic after our class party, Mr. Chips pushes the book he'd been perusing toward me and barks, "Happy Valentine's Day, Jeff!"

"Don't break any more of Miss Sea's precious keepsakes, please, Mr. Chips!" I admonish him, as he wags his tail and follows me from the attic, down the stairs and out the front doors of North School.

It has been an exciting Valentine's Day with my class. I have taken the heat for Mr. Chips' reckless transgressions. For a vexatious marauder, he is adorable, my little mischievous barking puppy, especially on Valentine's Day, when he has been the most problematical of puppies.

CHAPTER THREE: MARCH 17 AND ST. PATRICK'S DAY WITH MR. CHIPS

Mr. Chips is green with envy when he awakens me by licking the chartreuse-colored sock lint from between my toes early on St. Patrick's Day, then he jumps up onto his upholstered bed above the built-in toy storage cabinets located just below my bedroom windows.

He lets out a whole bunch of barks when he looks out and sees past the slats of the house ladder leaning out from the front exterior wall and above my windows, where he spies on our lawn, who else but Hazelnut, one of our beloved neighborhood chipmunks being chased around the yard by Oodles, my friend's frantic cat from next door, whose gray hair stands straight out and looks electrified, like the bride of Frankenstein.

"Don't run under the ladder, it's bad luck!" I

command of Mr. Chips as I dash downstairs to let my incorrigible puppy outside to join in all the fun in our front yard; and boy, is that a big mistake because he runs right under and all around the ladder, which pretty much guarantees bad luck will befall him today!

Despite the risk of an unlucky outcome from Mr. Chips foolishly running under the ladder and ignoring such a commonly held superstition, it hasn't really occurred to me what *might* happen when Hazelnut the chipmunk, Oodles the cat and my puppy all simultaneously notice *that ladder*. It is the very same ladder that Alec and Adolph had coincidentally purchased from Wienecke's Hardware in the village just the day before, darn it! It was just waiting there, leaning against the house in front of my second-floor bedroom and the perfect device to be employed as an escape route.

It really annoys me when I think about it that my older brother and stepfather had thoughtlessly gone inside the day before without finishing their gutter cleaning project just to watch a silly old golf match telecast from Florida on television; and had dangerously left the metal ladder leaned up against the front of the house, allowing diverted rainwater and the last of the winter snowmelt to continue dripping onto Mother's prized tulip beds, which are so soaked that they aren't a comfortable place for Hazelnut and her friend Johnnie the squirrel to sleep upon at night.

When I climb onto my chiffonier to get a better view of the front yard from out of my bedroom window, I see Hazelnut run up the ladder, followed ferociously by Oodles and then clumsily by Mr. Chips, who is barking madly as he stumbles up the metal stairs.

Next, Hazelnut, having reached the roof, jumps right off it onto a maple tree branch nearby just as Oodles is about to grab her and tumble into the tulip bed below. But Oodles neither grabs Hazelnut nor tumbles into the flowerbed. Instead, Oodles next jumps onto the maple tree branch near the corner of the house by Mother's bedroom and continues her pursuit; and with both Oodles and Hazelnut scrambling about on the large maple tree next door, Mr. Chips is left stranded, abandoned, trapped, desolate and stuck high up on the roof, alone and barking like a mad puppy while waking up the next-door neighbors at dawn; what fun!

By the time Mr. Chips frighteningly realizes that it's far easier for a puppy to climb a ladder than descend one, his barking causes Mother to check out all the drama unfolding outside; meanwhile, everyone in our house has been awakened by all the infernal racket outdoors and Mother has called the fire department for an animal rescue operation.

"You kids stay off that ladder and do not try and rescue Mr. Chips please!" she says, as the fire truck pulls up surprisingly fast to our house. Mr. Chips keeps barking away, waking the entire neighborhood on St. Patrick's Day!

The neighbors come out in their pajamas and bathrobes to watch as Joe the fireman climbs the ladder; but Mr. Chips would have none of it and keeps barking until Fred, the Chief, offers him a tasty bribe of a puppy biscuit, which does the trick.

Mr. Chips barks, then saunters across the roof along the gutter and enjoys the biscuit until the fire chief nabs him and brings him down the ladder in his arms, saying, "Happy St. Patrick's Day to you all!" while he hands Mr. Chips to me and I squeeze him gently and add, "don't run up the ladder onto our roof ever again, Mr. Chips, especially on St. Patrick's Day!"

Mr. Chips lets out a squeal and a bark and promptly falls asleep cradled in my arms after an eventful morning.

I at last see Oodles chasing Hazelnut into the ravine where the little stream gurgles away quietly, its waters purling alongside the bluebells and tulips which duck in the wind as the cat and chipmunk celebrate the holiday by chasing each other throughout the underbrush. All is well once again in our little Glencoe neighborhood, as delightful a place as in any fairytale.

CHAPTER FOUR:
APRIL FOOLS
WITH MR. CHIPS

On April Fool's Day, we are playing spring croquet with Mr. Chips, who is graciously shagging the balls for us on the lawn when, suddenly, Mr. Chips takes off for our backyard neighbors' steep ravine, and then he disappears through the intervening bluebells and birch trees that surround the little rivulet which flows toward a drainage sewer north of Dundee Road.

"What's gotten into Mr. Chips?" I query Alec and his friend Morley Skolsky. They both shrug and look puzzled. I just think that they are clueless.

When we go to look for Mr. Chips in the ravine, we hear a whimpering bark come from inside the drainage tunnel at the top of the ravine and located within the underbrush below our backyard neighbors' kitchen window.

"I'm stuck in here!" I hear Mr. Chips bark weakly; and when we peer inside the darkened narrow tunnel, it sure looks like Mr. Chips is scared and *indeed stuck* behind a trapped branch. He is virtually unreachable in the chiaroscuro interstices past the entry that are obscured by the tunnel's dim penumbra.

Alec and I discuss the delicate situation with Morley and we three conclude that the danger of attempting an inchoate rescue requires instead calling for professional reinforcements, especially after having my stepfather Adolph take a look; and he agrees that it appears as if Mr. Chips is really stuck inside the tunnel beneath a particularly gnarly large branch which has gotten jammed inside of the tunnel in a recent flooding downpour, although how *that* could happen, none of us can fathom.

Next, in consultation with the three others of us, I agree to have Adolph call the animal welfare department and the village police to jointly come out to our Elm Ridge neighborhood and see what advice they have to offer and to determine if they can rescue my puppy Mr. Chips, who keeps barking every so often.

Even at nine years of age, I am centered and in command of my own faculties and emotions in a difficult situation like this one. I maintain my composure and am very deliberate in my actions. And that's why I succeed. I have learned how to be proactive from watching how the older men who are role models in my family have accomplished so much.

****

When Officer Nildo shows up, he has brought a long pole with a set of rubber tipped clamps attached to it which he skillfully uses with my encouragement to dislodge the branch blocking Mr. Chips egress from the tunnel, then he places a bowl of puppy biscuits which I agree to use as an enticement at the front of the tunnel opening where we are squatting; and lo and behold, Mr. Chips barks and prances out of the tunnel, still barking and stopping to grab a complimentary biscuit before he jumps into my arms.

I declare, "'All's well that ends well', even on April Fool's Day!" joyously paraphrasing the poet.

While Morley, Alec and Adolph smile, I say, "thank you Officer Naldo—!"

"That's *Nildo*, son!" the officer interrupts, correcting me.

"Gotcha, April Fool's, officer!" I chortle as Mr. Chips lets out a cute little bark of agreement.

CHAPTER FIVE:
MAY 10 AND
MOTHER'S DAY
WITH MR. CHIPS

Mother's Day dinner 1959 is going to be celebrated with the family at Emerald Isles Country Club in Northbrook and I have to have my best navy blue Brooks Brothers suit on in the evening; but before that, I have all day for fun *and* time for a celebratory lunch with Mr. Chips and Mother in the city. But where would we celebrate? There is only *one place, of course!*

"Paul!" Mother requests of our chauffeur, "please get the limousine ready to take us to Marshall Field's department store on State Street!"

When we are ready and waiting for the chauffeur in the library, Paul comes in with his black suit and cap with the shiny visor.

Mr. Chips trots in with a handsome tartan plaid sweater jacket, a mauve hat with a robin's eggshell blue feather and a pink bow around his neck.

Mother, always elegantly dressed, is wearing a silver St. John's knit suit and I am sporting my new navy-blue Brooks Brothers suit with a pink Hermes tie. We are all styling, even Mr. Chips!

****

Paul drives us the scenic route along Sheridan Road, passing the mansions and castles of the rich and famous who live along the storied thoroughfare as it winds its way through Winnetka, Kenilworth and finally Wilmette, where we pass the Baha'I Temple, a giant concrete Faberge egg-looking structure of intricate design which glows from within its thousands of interstices.

When we reach the famed 'Gold Coast' of the city, we turn east onto Lake Shore Drive, which skirts the sparkling sapphire waters of Lake Michigan as we drive past Wyler Memorial Hospital, which honors the legacy of Grandpa Wyler's generosity.

On and on Paul drives us toward the city and its Michigan Avenue skyline, which reminds me of the Emerald City of Oz. When we arrive at Marshall Field's flagship famous department store on State

Street, Paul pulls the Cadillac alongside the south side of the building and quickly gets out of the limousine to help us disembark while we are safely parked away from the traffic and under the porte cochere. Mother loves arriving there like a member of the nineteenth century carriage trade, even if we are showing up in a mid-twentieth century black Cadillac limousine.

Mr. Chips is strictly instructed to never bark inside of the famed department store so as to not disturb the tranquil ambience of the gilded age structure or its fancy North Shore and Michigan Avenue clientele. Thankfully Mr. Chips already knows about the decorum of the store from our earlier visits to Marshall Field's miniature store in Lake Forest; and when we show up at the State Street store and its iconic Walnut Room Restaurant upstairs, Mr. Chips sits on my lap quietly, munching on a liver snap puppy biscuit while Mother enjoys a Waldorf Salad and I have the restaurant's famous signature dish, an open face 'Field's Special' sandwich, including a slice of rye bread, sliced turkey, Swiss cheese, thousand island dressing with capers and an iced tea. It is great fun being with Mother and Mr. Chips at Marshall Field's.

After we enjoy our fun lunch, we take the elevator down to the ground floor, where we pass the cosmetics and perfume aisles, where I purchase Mother a small bottle of Chanel No. 5, her favorite scent.

Then, we walk out the south side of the building, where we find Paul, who is still waiting for us with the limousine at the porte cochere; and we tell him that we are going to take Mr. Chips for a stroll along State Street toward the Chicago River, along Wacker Drive West. Mother instructs our chauffeur to please drive the limousine over to meet us along River North at the corner of State Street and Illinois Street.

Mr. Chips, who's been a good puppy all day and has remained quiet during the entire time we are in the department store, finally lets out a bark of agreement with our itinerary; and when we arrive at the Chicago River and are halfway over the bridge, Mr. Chips looks down at the waterway and sees a tourist-filled sightseeing riverboat getting ready to depart from its moorings. Some of the tourists wave and call out to us in good humor, Mr. Chips hears them, then suddenly and without warning pulls away from his leash and dashes over to the stairs leading down to the water, scampers down the steps and jumps onboard the riverboat to the applause and laughter of the throng of onboard tourists just as the boat inauspiciously leaves the dock.

"Wait!" I call out to the captain, as the riverboat heads west toward the Merchandise Mart and the junction with the North Branch of the

Chicago River, "my puppy, Mr. Chips is on your sightseeing boat! Please stop, Mr. Captain!"

I backtrack on the bridge toward the loop and run along Wacker Drive West toward the Merchandise Mart, with Mother chasing me, clearly distraught. By that time, the chauffeur Paul serendipitously has spotted us, turned around the waiting limousine on State Street just north of the river, then speeds west along 'the Drive' in pursuit of us, arriving at the exact sightseeing spot along the river by the Merchandise Mart where the tourist boat has thankfully already stopped.

By that point, I have already caught up with the parked tourist boat, Mr. Chips is barking up a storm and the captain officially hands him back over to me, miraculously with his leash still attached.

In a disciplinary tone, Mother says, "Jeffrey Joseph, don't ever run off like that again!" She maternally squeezes me and my puppy while we walk up the riverfront stairs to the front of the Merchandise Mart as the tourists on board the riverboat applaud us in unison.

"Happy Mother's Day!" I say to Mother, adding "now, Mr. Chips, behave yourself!" I command, as my puppy lets out an adorable bark and I squeeze him and say to the cutest puppy in the whole world, "'all's well that ends well', once again, Mr. Chips!" on a Happy Mother's Day.

****
****

Later that evening during buffet dinner at Emerald Isles, Sharon asks, "how was lunch at the Walnut Room?"

Mother answers in her inimitable deadpan voice, always cutting right to the chase with an economy of words, "just fine dear!"

"Anything interesting happen today?" Alec asks me.

"It was just a quiet Mother's Day lunch at Marshall Field's Walnut Room downtown in the loop!" I say as Mother looks at me knowingly and nods in quiet agreement, laughing out loud, "yes, it was all just lovely!" she responds.

The hectic travails of the day were our little secret; and one best kept that way between Mother and son!

Once again, Happy Mother's Day!

CHAPTER SIX: JUNE 1 AND CHILDREN'S DAY WITH MR. CHIPS

Children's Day brings bright June sunshine and warm temperatures to our Glencoe neighborhood; and I decide that the day is a fine day to take Mr. Chips for a walk into the village, where we could visit some of our most favorite stores, including Miller's Delicatessen, Wieneckes Hardware, Fells Clothing and The Surprise Shop.

"Mr. Chips!" I ask him in the kitchen, "do you want to join me for a walk into town today?"

"Yes please!" I hear him bark to me, while the maid, Carol, and the butler, Paul, just hear a simple bark in return. "I'm having my breakfast first!" Mr. Chips barks, as I see him wearing a small, checked bib and enjoying the food in his metal dish on a diminutive table with its own placemat a couple of inches off the floor.

After I have my Wheaties and a glass of orange juice, I brush and floss my teeth and gargle with Listerine for that 'fresh from the dentist office' clean tingling feeling.

Mr. Chips has by now gotten ready for our walk and is accoutered with mirrored sunglasses, black shiny booties and sporting a light pale blue windbreaker with a broad brimmed straw hat upon his head that has a clear dark emerald visor in front. He is all ready for his fun day of shopping on the Children's Day holiday.

With him on a long leash, I escort Mr. Chips through our back door neighbor's yard where my friend Cara lives; and she happens to come out the door by their kitchen, when she sees us and says, "can I join you and Mr. Chips on a walk this morning?"

"Sure, Cara!" I say cheerfully, "we're heading into town this morning, and you are welcome to join us!"

We head south on Bluff to Dundee Road, then head east to Grove, where we cross the thoroughfare, being careful to look both ways, after which we enter the small pocket park that stretches along the south side of Dundee Road between Grove Street and Greenleaf Street, a heavily wooded setting with a small tan bark and swing set enclosure and a little asphalt path which winds through the diminutive woods in such a manner that, in the summer, it feels very isolated, though the park is only the size of a couple village house lots.

As Cara and I and Mr. Chips walk along the deserted path through the woods, a sudden burst of summer wind blows through the trees and startles Mr. Chips into barking, "I don't like this park at all!" as we walk out onto Greenleaf Street and head south toward Park Avenue and the village center over by the Chicago and Northwestern railroad tracks.

As we stroll midway down Greenleaf Street, we approach a house with a scraggly copse in front that looks like an old beaten down wooden cottage, more like a large shack than a house, with an outdoor covered porch raised up three steps off the ground, a spooky place even in the sunshine.

A large oak tree along the sidewalk suddenly shakes in the wind, a flock of pigeons fly out of the canopy, startling us and Mr. Chips, who lets out another bark; and then I hear a feral growl from inside the shack, and I say to Cara, "let's get outta here!" as we take off toward Park Avenue, then hightail it east to the village and the Surprise Shop, where the proprietress, seeing us, immediately comes to the door and opens it up to show us the toy treasures which fill the bay windows, the shelves along the walls and the myriad barrels scattered about the entirety of the small shop, several of which are filled with the store's famous 'surprise balls', softball sized trinket-filled ribbon-wrapped delights.

"Hi, Joel!" Cara says to the shy boy who walks in behind us, as she whispers to me, "he's so nice, but his older brothers who live with him in that shack on Greenleaf *aren't* so nice!"

"Hi Cara and Jeff!" he says in a friendly manner, surprisingly.

"Hi Joel!" I respond as I look around at the dazzling array of toys and games.

From Candyland to Yahtzee, there was a cornucopia of toys and games to marvel at; and Cara and I have a great time in the store until Mr. Chips lets out a warning bark as three boys whom I assume are Joel's older brothers and all a little older than us walk by. With them is a big German shepherd who lets out the feral growl we'd heard earlier at the shack on Greenleaf; but I'm not scared because we are inside the most magical store in the whole world, the Surprise Shop, and we are as safe there as in a Grimm's fairy tale castle.

After Cara and I have our fill of looking at the sparkling gimcracks and showy gewgaws at the toy store, Mr. Chips barks and we say our pleasant goodbyes and thanks to Miss Prim, the proprietress and to Joel too, then Cara and I stroll arm-in-arm next door to look in at the windows of Fells, the clothing emporium, where we see some bathing suits and decide to tell each of our mothers that they look real nice.

We then walk across Park Avenue from the village library and stop in at Mr. Ricky's, where Mr. Chips claims everyone's attention by letting out a bark. We get complimentary Nestle Crunches there and later, Green Rivers at Millers, followed by our purchases of trading cards at Wieneckes, after which we march north on Vernon Avenue, purposely bypassing Greenleaf Street to the west where the spooky house is located; and as we walk alongside the property of North Shore Congregation, we see the three boys and their large German Shepard following us again, but Joel is not with them.

Discretion being the better part of valor, we hightail it across Dundee Road to Sunset Lane and quickly ditch the three older boys and their big dog too.

Mr. Chips lets out a cute bark just as we turn west off of Vernon Avenue and onto Sunset Lane, as if to say, 'na na nuh na na' once we are safely on our neighborhood turf. Cara and I don't let the mean boys and their dog spoil our perfectly lovely day in the village; and their younger brother Joel has been very nice, anyway.

****

Oh, and I forgot to mention that we each have been given a gift at the toy store: — one surprise ball for Cara, another for me and a squeeze toy stuffed animal of 'Lassie' for Mr. Chips; all gifts from Miss Prim on Children's Day 1959. How perfectly sublime life can be as a kid growing up in Glencoe!

CHAPTER SEVEN: JULY 4TH WITH MR. CHIPS!

July 4th is always the most fun holiday of the year because Alec, Sharon and I get to stay up late that night to watch the fireworks; and the 1959 celebration would be extra special because the fireworks would be held just off the beachfront at the east end of Park Avenue and down the steeply graded pedestrian walkway that lead to the stairs by the sandy shore of Lake Michigan.

Mr. Chips remains excited all day, barking outside at Mother's arrogant roses and delightful lilacs, who aren't having any of his braggadocio.

"I'm being taken to the beach this evening!" he barks on the tan bark, while the lilacs sniff their haughtily fragrant disapproval in the sunshine.

"We don't care!" they whisper in the wind.

Over at the roses, they hold their arms akimbo and shake their thorns at the effrontery of Mr. Chips' teasing them because *they too* aren't included in the evening's festivities.

"Did you want to come with us?" Mr. Chips barks at the Queen of the roses, the tallest most indignant of the bunch, "all we need to do is just trim you a little —!" he barks.

"How dare you?" the Queen of the roses responds to him indignantly, "we roses don't care a petal about your silky holiday!" the mad Queen concludes arrogantly.

"I think you meant to say that you don't care a fig, not a petal, about our silly, not our silky, 'holiday'!" Mr. Chips barks tendentiously at the prickly flower.

"How dare you talk back to me? Whatever!" the mad Queen shouts argumentatively, turning beet red as the lilacs nearby curtsy deferentially to the Queen in a coordinated gavotte as they bow in unison from a sudden gust of warm wind out of the west.

"Be off with you, Mr. Officious!" the lilacs whisper as a murmuration of starlings are startled from their purchase in the rambling hedge by the tanbark while Mr. Chips trots off imperiously, a majestic look of insolence upon his demeanor as he lifts one hind leg and pardons himself liquidaciously all over the charming rose bushes, who try their thorny best to smack him insolently in the breeze for his effrontery and disrespect; but only end up losing several of their precious petals instead.

"How dare you spray your graffiti upon us?" the mad Queen reacts angrily, "now be off with you before someone does the same to you, you pusillanimous little twit!" she yells.

"Why, that's quite improbable!" Mr. Chips barks in a very diplomatic tone, "and Happy July 4th holiday to you ladies!"

Mr. Chips continues barking at the intransigent flowers on his way around front, as they all ignore him, shake and look away, whispering, "that importunate dunderhead; why, he's simply incorrigible!" which the Queen agrees with, as her ladies-in-waiting, a sprig of pink roses, crowd around her and toss their heads insolently in the warm westerly wind.

****

After a nap and a nice dinner in the kitchen, Mr. Chips is dressed and ready to join us for a fun night out at the beach. It is a little cool and breezy, so he is sporting a silver windbreaker, a captain's cap and appropriate footwear, his specially made miniature Wellingtons, perfect for the beach. He looks like he is going on a cruise!

"Nice 'Wellies'" I say to him as he barks in the affirmative.

We all pile into Adolph's shiny fire engine red Buick convertible and drive over to the Park Avenue parking lot on the ridge high above the beach, after which Mr. Chips scampers ahead of us and down the pedestrian walkway, disappearing in the gloaming and around the corner of the steep drive where the stairs lead to the sand.

When we all get down to the beach, Mr. Chips is nowhere to be seen, which is typical because he is *always* disappearing.

When we look out at the lake, which is brightened at the beach by temporary floodlights set up just for the occasion, we can see a miniature elegant yacht, a replica of Mrs. Dodge's gorgeous *Delphine,* on which we can see Mr. Chips and his friends, a real doggone party boat; and they are laughing and barking themselves silly while enjoying their 'Shirley Temple' cocktails and mock-tails.

Mr. Chips as captain is clearly doing an admirable job of steering the miniature yacht far enough away from the location of the intended fireworks for safety purposes; but nobody could figure out how he has single-handedly arranged for the vessel; however, rumor has it at the beach that he is very tight with the proprietress of the Surprise Shop, and a model toy boat suspiciously just like it had been for sale in the bay window of her famed bodega for nearly a thousand dollars, a gigantic amount of money for us kids in 1959.

Mr. Chips is known to be very resourceful and probably acquired it on loan from Miss Prim in exchange for advertising its use on the lakefront. And with all the parents and their kids out on the beach seeing the spectacular toy boat float by, it is the promotional coup of the summer for the Surprise Shop.

"Is that the famous cartoon beagle on board?" Alec asks me as he squints out at the yacht in the distance.

"No, silly, that's our neighbor Judy's beagle; and he's just as real as Mr. Chips!" I announce seriously as the first of the fireworks explodes far out from the shoreline.

It is a gorgeous evening; and as the fireworks light up the sky, I think to myself, 'Mr. Chips always gets the best seat in the house, and he doesn't need a famous beagle's connections to pull it off!'

CHAPTER EIGHT: AUGUST 5TH AND 'WORK LIKE A DOG DAY' WITH MR. CHIPS!

"Judy called to invite you and Mr. Chips over to her pool today!" Mother announces when I follow my brother and sister downstairs for an early morning breakfast on the propitious morning of 'Work Like a Dog Day'.

"I'll have Kellogg's Corn Flakes please!" Sharon says.

"May I have half a grapefruit, a piece of toast and a sunny side up egg please?" Alec asks.

"I'd like a poached egg over a piece of buttered toast please!" I chime in.

"Coming up!" Paul the butler says, as his wife, Carol, the housekeeper says, "it'll be ready in just a few, kids!"

"If they ever leave!" Mother whispers, "we'll have to go to self-serve! You just can't get good help like them anymore!"

Mr. Chips barks in agreement.

"Everyone's replaceable except you and the kids, darling!" Adolph calls from the house entryway, where he is putting on a windbreaker on his way to an early morning golf game at Emerald Isles.

"What's everyone up to today?" Mother asks, as Alec and Sharon say simultaneously , "we're going sailing with Uncle Ralph today!"

"You owe me a Coke, brother!" Sharon says.

"I'm escorting Mr. Chips over to Judy's pool for the day!" I add, as Mr. Chips barks enthusiastically.

****

*****

After our hearty breakfast, I help Mr. Chips into his one-piece bathing suit, baseball cap, Foster Grants and Wellies for our short trek over to the neighborhood's most fabulous private garden, beautifully landscaped around a gorgeously manicured pool and patio setting.

By the time Mr. Chips and I arrive, all the kids on our block are there, including the most glamorous girls, Judy, Holly and Joanie, all of whom make a big fuss over Mr. Chips, the moment my celebrated puppy prances into the backyard enclosure.

Mr. Chips is immediately given a chaise lounge of honor under an umbrella, with a bowl of water and a basket of snacking biscuits next to him, as well as comic books featuring Rin Tin Tin and Lassie for his perusing pleasure.

"Does Mr. Chips want a beauty treatment and his nails done?" Holly graciously asks me.

"I'll let him make the call!" I answer, looking over at Mr. Chips.

Mr. Chips barks in the affirmative, as the most beautiful girls in my grammar school class fuss over him, trimming, clipping and polishing all his paw nails.

While I swim and play Marco Polo in the pool with the neighborhood boys, Mr. Chips is pampered with the very best in royal treatment offered by Judy, Holly, Joanie and the rest of the neighborhood girls.

When they are done with all their beauty treatments, Mr. Chips is the most glamorous schnauzer I've ever seen. And I've had fun all afternoon with my friends in the pool playing

Marco Polo and tossing a frisbee.

'Work Like a Dog Day' is the best day of the year 1959 for Mr. Chips because he's gotten to have the day off for his 'fun in the sun' while all the kids in the neighborhood have treated him like a prince. Kudos to you, Mr. Chips, on this and every holiday!

CHAPTER NINE: SEPTEMBER 7 AND LABOR DAY WITH MR. CHIPS!

With Mother and the ladies scheduled to play Canasta on Labor Day, the rest of the family takes advantage of the nice weather and warm temperatures to drive to Sportsmen's Park and practice our golf swings. With Adolph in the driver's seat, Alec, Sharon, Mr. Chips and I all pile into our stepfather's shiny new lipstick-red Buick convertible. My older brother and sister are almost always busy doing other things, so this is a truly special day to celebrate us all being together on a fun outing.

Alec is already learning how to golf with Adolph at Emerald Isles Country Club in Northbrook, located a little east of Sportsmen's Park, where we're going to rent a bucket of golf balls today for each of us. That way, we'll be ready next season for that tough course at the club.

Even Mr. Chips gets in the act here at Sportsmen's with his miniature set of golf clubs and fancy white leather golf shoes. But what really surprises us is that, when Adolph opens up the car trunk, he pulls out a small electric golf cart on the back of which he places Mr. Chips' golf bag and clubs; and off Mr. Chips goes to the miniature golf course and putting green in a puff of blue smoke, wearing his clear green visor and Scottish plaid golf outfit while smoking a fancy Montecristo Cuban cigar.

Mr. Chips takes his golf game very seriously, especially on Labor Day, traditionally the last day of summer vacation.

****

Later on, our holiday picnic dinner is not complete until Mr. Chips barks his approval in our backyard that he is satisfied with his personal hot diggity dog, grilled on a miniature grill just for him and prepared by Carol and Paul from his very own specially prepared puppy chow; how nice!

We all enjoy our family dinner, play a game of croquet afterwards and then watch Mr. Chips chase fireflies around the yard. The sun, a giant tangerine orb, sets in the cobalt western sky, which has gradually turned a midnight velvet blue amidst the twinkling diamond stars of another fun Labor Day night of 1959 in Glencoe!

CHAPTER TEN: OCTOBER 31 AND HALLOWEEN WITH MR. CHIPS

What would Halloween and my birthday be without great costumes? Mr. Chips and I know just who we want to be: — why, Sherman and Mr. Peabody, of course!

We dress up like our favorite cartoon characters from 'Rocky and Bullwinkle' on television. Once Alec and Sharon are ready, we meet Morley, Davie and Sadie Skolsky over at their place on Bluff Street.

Their home reminds me of the disheveled mansion in the famous movie, *Sunset Boulevard;* and it is a perfectly spooky place to begin our trick-or-treating odyssey on the scariest night of the year, when all the ghosts and goblins are flying about our ten-square-block neighborhood, which seems to cover our entire kids' world.

Both Mr. Chips and I wear the trademark glasses with thick black frames of Mr. Peabody and Sherman; and whenever an adult opens his or her front door to hand us candy and squawk at us, they also marvel at the famous cartoon characters we are impersonating.

The others in our group are all characters from Oz, including Alec as the tin man, Morley as the scarecrow and Davie as the lion; while the two girls are Sadie dressed as Dorothy with her ruby slippers and Sharon as Auntie Em.

The girls prefer Mr. Chips as Toto; but he barks his wish to be Mr. Peabody, and on Halloween, Mr. Chips gets to do what *he wants to do!*

Come to think of it, Halloween is no different than any other day because Mr. Chips always does *whatever he wants!*

****

We endure vintage Halloween storm season weather: — blustery windy spooky and rainy. We trudge through snow flurries, icy slush and leaves falling like scary goblins and ghosts from the gnarly blackened denuded trees. But every house with a light on at the front door is a refuge from the chilly damp wind. And the friendly faces, smiles and candy of all the kindly old homeowners who greet us are welcome sights, making our journey in the nasty weather worth every minute of the wonderful time we six kids have together on glorious Halloween night.

****

As we say goodnight to our friends after a *long* night making the rounds of the entire neighborhood trick-or-treating and finally part ways on our journey home from the Skolsky mansion on Bluff Street, I hear Mr. Chips bark 'Happy Halloween to all; and, to all, a goodnight!'

The Skolsky kids wave goodbye from their front door as we cut through the spooky backyard of our neighbors and sneak in through the back door of our house to marvel at all our edible treasures on the kitchen table. A king's ransom wouldn't have held more fascination for me, my brother and sister than the treasures we've acquired during our night of rambling about our Glencoe neighborhood.

Halloween 1959 has been really the most perfect night of the year, especially because we've been with Mr. Peabody,— er;— I mean, Mr. Chips, of course, on my tenth birthday!

CHAPTER ELEVEN: NOVEMBER 26TH AND THANKSGIVING WITH MR. CHIPS

M r. Chips and I know just how we want to celebrate Thanksgiving Day lunch: — why, at the new McDonalds with a 'drive-through' in Northbrook, of course, with my older brother and older sister joining us and Mother driving everyone in her new fancy pale blue 'T' Bird convertible!

Thanksgiving dinner will be at home later. The whole family will be there, including all my cousins, aunts and uncles and even my Grandma Pearlie. Everybody will be all dressed up for the fancy occasion; and Mother will serve turkey, of course, and stuffing, sweet potatoes and cranberry mold, vanilla ice cream and pumpkin pie for dessert. It will be simply glorious!

But before all the evening festivities, Mr. Chips and I have to gather everyone in the late morning to drive us to McDonald's for a hamburger, French fried potatoes and a chocolate milk shake.

Mr. Chips is very excited about our outdoor excursion and runs around the entire house barking his head off with joy.

After he has nearly worn himself out from all his running about, he barks loudly enough that I know he wants to go out in the backyard before lunch and play with his friends, Oodles the cat and Hazelnut's friend Johnnie the squirrel, whom Mr. Chips chases around the yard; Oodles finally dashing into and disappearing deep within the storm drain tunnel at the head of the ravine and Hazelnut joining Johnnie in scrambling up one of the gigantic maple trees in back.

After all that excitement, Mr. Chips trots in for his bath in the laundry room sink, soaking in warm water with a smidgen of mild Dove soap while perusing the latest *Look* magazine, after which I towel him off and help him don a pair of khaki trousers and a bright plaid shirt with a gray windbreaker and an earth toned scarf, all handcrafted just for him, special order, at Fells in the village.

We are all ready for our adventure to McDonalds, with Alec and Sharon in the 'T' Bird backseats, Mother driving and Mr. Chips in my lap in the front passenger seat, barking for us to get a move-on!

Mother backs the robin's eggshell blue 'T' Bird out of the garage and drives us down Elm Ridge to Dundee Road, heads west to Waukegan Avenue and North to just past County Line, where one of the first drive through McDonalds in the nation is located.

We each get our usual hamburger, French fried potatoes and a chocolate shake, of course. Mr. Chips is treated to something he can enjoy too, because I have crafted little puppy treats that look like miniature hamburgers, just for him; and he loves them while barking his approval.

Thanksgiving dinner that evening will be memorable as always; but nothing is more fun than all of us going to McDonalds for a little holiday lunch with Mr. Chips, who finishes his meal in the parking lot, just the same as us, then proceeds to bark all the way home until he finally falls asleep in my lap as we pull into the garage after another fun adventure in Mother's special 1959 'T' Bird!

Happy Thanksgiving to all!

CHAPTER TWELVE: DECEMBER 25TH AND CHRISTMAS WITH MR. CHIPS!

Christmas Eve finds me and Mr. Chips looking at all the toys still on display at the old Surprise Shop in the village.

When he disappears into the store while I am checking out Parker Brothers *Monopoly* board game in the bay window, I see three men in dark pinstripe suits chatting with Miss Prim; but I search all over the place and can't find Mr. Chips until I scour the corner with the stuffed animals, and the only one whose eyes follow me and who lets out a bark when he sees me is Mr. Chips, who is clutching a 'Chatty Cathy' doll, which Miss Prim, the store proprietress, immediately insists that we take home, after which she wraps it up like a pretty Christmas gift for my older sister Sharon, whom she says has come into the store all season long staring at the doll and pulling its chain in her backside to make her speak.

"The three gentlemen from Mattel would like to give Mr. Chips their business cards and would like to schedule a meeting with him and his owner!" Miss Prim says, as Mr. Chips barks in the affirmative and I say, "sure, I'll check with Mother!"

I thank Miss Prim, Mr. Chips barks his approval once more and we each bike home on our separate Schwinn bicycles; I on my big boy one, and Mr. Chips on his itty bitty one with training wheels.

When we get home, I give the present to our maid Carol to give to Santa, so that he can deliver it to Sharon the very next day on Christmas. I want to see the look on her face when she opens the doll's toy box to see the glamorous Chatty Cathy; and after a restless sleep on Christmas Eve, my brother Alec, Mr. Chips and I dash downstairs with Sharon to see the Christmas tree all sparkling, with a toy town of gifts, presents and packages, around which chugs *Thomas the Train* on one track and *The Little Engine That Could* on an inner track in the opposite direction.

Sharon makes a dash for the big box holding the doll; and when she opens it up and sees Chatty Cathy, she pulls the cord in back and the doll starts talking to her like a friend and proceeds to ask her a series of questions.

Sharon is mesmerized by the lifelike doll and says, "Happy Holidays to you Jeff and to you too Alec!"

After I enjoy a wonderful Christmas morning with Alec and Sharon and I've opened up all of my many presents and put them neatly stored away in my room in my toy storage cabinets beneath my bedroom windows, I could see that it is snowing heavily outside as I look over at the most special gift of all I had received, a framed picture standing upon the corner of my desk from Mother.

Bathed in the soft light of the desk lamp and within the framed glass enclosed picture is a small drawing and a separate note below it. Mother has beautifully designed a proper framed enclosure and stand for the priceless drawing and had it fabricated, courtesy of the Glencoe Stationery Shop on Vernon Avenue. The small drawing is a whimsical depiction of the scene which I had described in my simple letter to Mr. Rockwell and mailed to his art gallery representatives the past Valentine's Day.

The image of the drawing shows a street corner, a streetlamp with missing panes shattered on the ground, a policeman looking at two boys and a small puppy with a quizzical stare who is looking back at the officer while snow flurries fall.

I know that scene is of us, of course!

Within the glass enclosed frame and beneath the sketch is a brief note, which reads as follows, and I quote:— 'Dear Jeff, the scene you described, while poignant, was unfortunately not chosen to be reprinted by *The Post*, but I thought you might like it just the same as a small token of my appreciation for your efforts in informing me of this unique slice of your life. Please stay safe and out of trouble. Don't throw snowballs at another streetlamp. And Merry Christmas to you and your family! Norman.'

****

We never threw another snowball at a streetlamp ever again, honest Injun! And all I can add to that is, 'Merry Christmas to all, and to all, a good night', from me and Mr. Chips to you!

BOOK IV: MISTER CHIPS TAKES NEW YORK CITY BY STORM!

CHAPTER ONE:
THE PLAZA HOTEL

Christmas 1959

The day of the Vetch family trip from Glencoe to New York City had finally arrived; and it was a perfect day for an airplane flight, a bright sunny crisp day, with the latest snowfall blanketing their Glencoe backyard in a pretty coat of white on the day after Christmas, in the year 1959.

Paul, the Vetch's tall handsome African American chauffeur, had the black Cadillac limousine polished and the family's luggage was all packed in the trunk and ready to go. What a day it would be!

After saying their goodbyes to the cook and Paul's wife, Carol, who was in the kitchen, the family, including Dr. and Mrs. Vetch and their three children, Alec, the oldest; next, Sharon; and the youngest, Jeff, who was charged with holding their prized miniature German schnauzer, Mr.

Chips, in his arms, all returned to the library.

When Paul was ready for them, the family exited through the hall leading from the library to the mansion's garage; and, with Paul holding the back door of the automobile directly behind the passenger seat open, everyone in the family ducked in, one by one, to enter the limousine's capacious back seating lounge, with Dr. And Mrs. Vetch sitting in the very back and facing forward, and across from them, Sharon, Alec and Jeff with Mr. Chips in his lap, all three of whom had their backs to the rolled up limousine window separating the chauffeur from the family.

Dolores Vetch noted to her youngest son, "my word, Jeffrey Joseph, Mr. Chips is *very formally* dressed today, with his navy-blue blazer, pink Hermes bow tie, Ferragamo loafers on his paws and cobalt mirror Ray-Ban shades!"

"Yes, he is!" Jeff agreed proudly, patting Mr. Chips lightly on his back.

Paul carefully backed the limousine out of the garage, down the driveway and around Elm Ridge to Dundee Road, where he headed east to Sheridan Road over by Lake Michigan.

"Dolores, remember, Mr. Chips is on his way to being a big hitter now!" Dr. Vetch noted, as Mr. Chips remained silent, cool and aloof; the unmistakable traits of a rising star.

"I'm not sure if he's a big hitter quite yet!" Jeff responded, while Mr. Chips remained silent on the matter.

"I'll bet he *will be* after *this* trip!" Alec announced.

"I wouldn't be surprised!" Sharon chimed in.

"Nor would I!" Dr. Vetch added.

"Yes, as I've said numerous times, kids, there's always room at the top for one more success! But I'm still not sure if Mr. Chips deserved a trust fund when we set them up for the children!"

"Nobody *deserves* a trust fund dear; but you've done pretty doggone well with yours!" Adolph mentioned.

"Mr. Chips'll do doggone well too!—" Jeff added.

"That's because of the expertise of the family money managers and lawyers!" Mrs. Vetch stated, interrupting her youngest son, "not me or my influence," Mrs. Vetch noted, as the gleaming ebony colored limousine glided past the great mansions along Sheridan Road, from southeast Glencoe through the ravines of Winnetka and on into Kenilworth and the Plaza Del Lago.

"Yes, dear, your money managers at Stein

Roe and your lawyer Bob Alt have done a uniformly superb job!" Dr. Vetch said to his wife.

"I still think a trust fund for Mr. Chips was a bit much, even if he's a far sharper cookie than the average pooch!" Mrs. Vetch noted, as the limousine headed through the north side of the city and then onto Lake Shore Drive, where the automobile glided past Wyler Memorial Hospital, an institution funded by Mrs. Vetch's mother Pearlie in memory of her legendary husband Lawrence Wyler, who was an enormously successful early and mid-twentieth century businessman who had garnered a substantial fortune in the liquor industry between the end of prohibition and the end of World War II.

"Mr. Chips doesn't exactly have a trust fund dear!" Dr. Vetch noted, as the limousine sped south along the outer drive past Belmont Harbor, where Lawrence Wyler, the family's fountainhead, had once kept his prized sailboat, *Rubyacht,* "Mr. Chips is a collateral residuary beneficiary just mentioned in a codicil to your Will with a small bequest for his care and sustenance, should the need ever arise, that's all, dear!"

"That's just fine!" Mrs. Vetch noted, as Mr. Chips at last let out a confirming bark of agreement with the arcane legalities of his financial security.

"Mr. Chips also has a full schedule of

meetings lined up in New York during our trip, doesn't he?" Sharon asked of Jeff, as the chauffeur drove past East Lake Shore Drive on the way to Midway Airport south of the Loop.

"Yes, he does, from the moment we arrive later today at the Plaza. Mother has Mr. Chips scheduled to meet the Mattel people tonight at the Champagne Bar at the hotel in order to discuss his brand-new line of *Mr. Chips!* branded and copyrighted stuffed animals, which are planned on being showcased initially at only very high-end and tony toy emporiums," Jeff said, as Mr. Chips remained taciturn and debonair, a cool cucumber if there ever was one.

"Tomorrow during the late morning, Mr. Chips is meeting the people at FAO Schwartz to review plans for a specially made miniature battery operated and long-distance driving cream-colored Rolls Royce Corniche convertible with a lipstick-red leather interior for his personal use as well as a promotional tour related to his eponymous stuffed animals," Dr. Vetch said.

"Yes; and Jeff, are you planning on accompanying Mr. Chips to all his events while we're in New York City?" Mrs. Vetch asked.

"Yes, I am, plus the Pinkerton security guard you've arranged for me who will also be accompanying us absolutely *everywhere*, Mother!" Jeff answered matter-of-factly.

"I don't care if your *Dick Tracy watch* can call out the United States marines and cavalry brigade, Jeffrey Joseph, you are *not going to be ever* wandering around the dangerous island of Manhattan alone and on your own, *period!*" Mrs. Vetch commanded imperiously.

"I wouldn't be alone. I'd be with Mr. Chips and Pinkerton security *at all times,* Mother," Jeff reiterated.

"I'll also be accompanying you whenever possible, dear!" Mrs. Vetch ordered in a somewhat more conciliatory tone.

"That's not necessary, Mother, because I know you want to sightsee, shop at Saks, see our paintings by Masson on loan to the Museum of Modern Art and visit Sidney Janis Gallery to see their *Homage to the Squares* series by Albers before Mr. Paley buys them all!" Jeff responded.

"That's all true; but I will also find time to be with you and Mr. Chips as you travel around New York City with the Pinkerton guard," Mrs. Vetch responded.

"You can never be *too safe* in New York City!" Dr. Vetch chimed in.

"That's certainly true!" Alec added.

"Let me know if I can help too!" Sharon said.

"I will certainly be accompanying you and

Mr. Chips all around New York City, Jeffrey Joseph, even with the guard present," Mrs. Vetch reiterated, continuing, "after all, you're only a kid of eight—!"

"Ten, Mother!" Jeff interrupted.

"Eight nine ten whatever years old, for goodness sake!" Mrs. Vetch continued, "you're just a kid; and a precious one, at that, dear."

"But mom!" Jeff said, looking at his stepfather.

"Now do as your mother says, she knows best, Jeff!" Dr. Vetch responded seriously.

"All right," Jeff conceded, adding, "then in the first evening," Jeff continued, as the chauffeur approached Midway Airport, "Mr. Chips is meeting the casting director from *My Fair Lady* at the Bemelmans Bar at the Carlyle to discuss the possibility of a one show only walk-on in the 'Ascot Races' scene of the play opposite Rex Harrison and Julie Andrews".

"Really?" Alec asked.

"Yes! The day after that, he's arranged to meet Bernard Baruch!" Jeff mentioned.

"Bernard Baruch?" Alec asked, sounding flabbergasted.

"Yes, the one and only, in Central Park over by the pond where the little sailboats are, in order to discuss blue chip stock investing with the proceeds of his percentage of the Mr. Chips trademarked stuffed animal sales!" Jeff concluded.

"Who knew he was such a big hitter!" Alec mentioned, as Mr. Chips snorted, removed a silver cigarette case from out of his breast pocket and then pulled out a cigarette, after which Dr. Vetch pulled out his Zippo lighter, lit the cigarette for Mr. Chips, who, with that certain air of 'je ne sais quoi' and film noir insouciance, took a deep drag and blew a puff of silver blue smoke toward Mrs. Vetch, enveloping her in a shimmering cloud while subtly exercising his influence over her without uttering so much as a bark.

Mr. Chips' unspoken air of superiority was striking for its authenticity, a characteristic usually reserved for those who are profoundly unpleasant; but in his case, it came off as more or less part of his breeding and atavistic charm.

"Mr. Chips has certainly adopted an air of 'tres chic' about him! That's quite a to-do list he's got to accomplish! Is that it?" Mrs. Vetch asked, her deadpan humor lost on cool Mr. Chips, who ignored her completely and appeared distantly focused on the outdoors beyond the limousine windows, his expression featureless behind his impenetrable shades.

"Oh no, Mother, there's more, much more, because Mr. Chips is meeting Ed Sullivan and Topo

LOUIS W.HIRSCHMANN

Gigio at either the Ritz or 21 Club after the theater later in the week, and they're firming it up with Mr. Chips' advertising agent at Ted Bates in New York as we speak!"

"He has an advertising agent?" Mrs. Vetch asked.

"Yes of course! His line of *Mr. Chips!* stuffed animals require advertising, marketing, product placement, etcetera!" Jeff stated seriously. Any Northwestern University marketing major worth his salt knows that!"

"Well, I suppose so!" Mrs. Vetch responded, "and is that where you're planning on going to graduate school?" she asked.

"If they'll consider me in about fifteen years in 1973, why yes, of course!" Jeff responded.

Looking over at cool, calm and collected Mr. Chips, who was sitting up and staring out the window on Jeff's lap, Mrs. Vetch added, 'well, I'm heartened to hear that Mr. Chips is doing so well in his business ventures, Jeff!" the matron of the family stated succinctly as the chauffeur pulled their long black limousine into Midway Airport's passenger unloading zone.

****

Several hours later following a quick flight and a hired limousine ride from Idlewood to Manhattan, the Vetches were at the famous Plaza Hotel at the corner of 59th and 5th in Manhattan.

"Adolph, be sure we get a high floor with connecting three-room corner-suites along 5th Avenue and the park, dear, including our bedroom, a private bedroom with an en-suite just for Sharon and a living room with a separate bathroom and two convertible beds for the boys along with a comfortable nook for Mr. Chips' privacy too," Mrs. Vetch stated.

"Yes, dear; but that'll be very expensive!" Dr. Vetch said.

"I don't care because that's what I want, dear!" Mrs. Vetch said to her husband.

"And I also want fifth row center for *My Fair Lady* and I don't care how much that costs either!" Mrs. Vetch added.

"Yes, dear; but remember, that'll cost a fortune too!" Dr. Vetch reminded her dutifully.

As the family was checking in at the hotel front desk, three blue suited men came up to Jeff and Mr. Chips, on whose collar Jeff had attached a sparkling multicolored bejeweled leash to keep him from running off in all the commotion of the busy lobby.

"Hello sirs!" Jeff said, adding, "I recognize you all from the Surprise Shop in Glencoe a couple of days ago this past Christmas Eve!"

"Nice to see you and your prized ward too, Jeff!" Mr. Niedelbaum said, adding, "you remember my Mattel associates Tom Sedgemore and Dick Roland too from the Surprise Shop?"

"Yes, sir!" Jeff said as he shook their hands.

After introductions were made and pleasantries exchanged, Jeff, Mrs. Vetch and the men from Mattel all strolled into the Plaza's famous Champagne Bar, while Dr. Vetch, Sharon and Alec finalized the family's suite assignments and the arrangements for the incredibly expensive theater tickets to the famous play *My Fair Lady* which they would be attending later in the week.

Dr. Vetch could be overheard walking through the lobby to the elevators and muttering, "a thousand dollars for tickets to the play; oh, my goodness!"

****

While Jeff marveled at the elegant informality of the stunning Plaza Champagne Bar, he also enjoyed a Buck Rogers, while Mrs. Vetch had a tonic and lime, Mr. Chips was presented with a silver bowl of Perrier mineral water which he sniffed, then tasted; and the three men from Mattel each had a J&B on the rocks with a lemon twist.

When Mr. Chips looked up from his Perrier drink toward the bar window facing Central Park, he noticed a beautiful red robin and her baby robin, both staring at him and chirping from the windowsill.

"We'd love to show you the park," the mama robin chirped, "I am Red Robin Barnard and my baby is Summer Rose; we're in the park by the sailboat pond every morning at ten am for the races and we'd love to show you around the place!" she chirped.

"Love to and we'll be there the day after tomorrow at the sailboat pond around ten a.m.!" Mr. Chips barked softly to Red Robin, who winked back at him and flew off with her baby northward toward the park as Jeff looked at Mr. Chips and scowled.

"Shhhhhh!" Jeff said, "you're in the Plaza now! Absolutely no barking if you please Mr. Chips, especially in the Champagne Bar!"

As they were all enjoying their aperitifs, the men from Mattel showed the Vetches various replicas of Mr. Chips stuffed animals as a puppy and prototypes as an adult schnauzer; and Mr.

Chips, with a twinkle of merriment in his ebony eyes, barked his hearty approval of the models right on the spot, with Jeff recommending that Mattel platform an initial small run of the dolls at FAO Schwartz and other fancy toy stores before doing a substantially larger national rollout.

"A brilliant idea, Jeff!" was the comment from the Mattel executives, with Mr. Chips echoing their sentiments with a congratulatory bark.

Th cocktail discussion ended with the Mattel executives agreeing to prepare all relevant legal documents concerning the *Mr. Chips!* brand project, comprising copyrights; the use of other media including radio, television, theatrical release and cinema; as well as Mr. Chips' initial signing bonus and his increasing scale percentage payments of gross sales at retail, all the precise documents for which would be mailed 'special delivery' to the Vetch family lawyers for their examination and ultimate sign off before making their final recommendations to the Vetch family on behalf of Mr. Chips.

"We'll see you at FAO tomorrow morning at ten am!" Jeff said, as Mrs. Vetch silently smiled, and Mr. Chips let out a congratulatory soft bark of acceptance with the proceedings at the Plaza.

"The Devil's in the details," Mrs. Vetch stated succinctly.

When they went to the front desk, Mrs. Vetch received her room keys and they went up to their corner suite, which comprised three exquisitely furnished large rooms in a grand French pale blue satin sea foam 'fin de siecle' style of matching bedspreads, couches and draperies, all of which were shimmering in the late afternoon sun. The capacious apartment suite was located on one of the hotel's mid-level floors, exactly where Mrs. Vetch had insisted, with views of the iconic corner at 59th and 5th on the seventh floor and commanding views of Central Park as well. For her, it was simply heaven on seven after a very long day of travel.

The family ordered room service and relaxed in their pajamas for the remainder of the evening, dining en-suite on shrimp cocktails, filet of Dover sole meunière and baby asparagus with a loaf of sliced French bread and butter and lime sherbet with fresh raspberries for dessert. It was a wonderful meal and a treat to dine en-suite overlooking Central Park.

"Get a good night's rest, everyone!" Mrs. Vetch recommended, "we've a busy day tomorrow!" she said.

"What about getting together at the Bemelmans Bar in the Carlyle with the casting director from *My Fair Lady* for Mr. Chips' one time walk-on?" Jeff asked.

"The director's assistant left a message at the front desk, and it's postponed, dear, for later in the week right at the theater!" Mrs. Vetch chimed in, adding, "it'll happen!"

CHAPTER TWO:
VISITING F A O
SCHWARTZ

The very next morning when Mr. Chips awakened, he saw his two new avian friends, Red Robin and Summer Rose, quietly chirping and looking into the Vetch corner living room from outside the hotel and right on the seventh-floor windowsill.

"I'll see you tomorrow morning!" Mr. Chips barked, as the two robins chirped their approval in response and flew north across 59th Street toward their home along Central Park West.

Awakening, Jeff said groggily, "shhhh, keep the barking down, Mr. Chips, you don't want to wake up the *whole* place, now do you?"

"You're doggone tootin' I do!" Mr. Chips barked back, as room service knocked on the living room door, awakening the rest of the family.

"I'm the only one in the whole world who can interpret your barks and understand you, Mr.

Chips!" Jeff whispered to his canine pal, who wagged his tail.

After the Vetches enjoyed a gorgeous room service breakfast exquisitely presented in the signature Plaza way, the family conducted their morning ablutions and dressed up in preparation for a fun and busy day in the city.

Alec, Sharon and Dr. Vetch were being picked up in the chauffeured limousine Dr. Vetch had arranged expressly for the purpose of driving them to see the art installation of surrealism at MOMA which included the family's famous painting *Pasiphae* by Andre Masson, on temporary loan to the museum.

Mrs. Vetch, Jeff and Mr. Chips were meeting the Pinkerton guard which Mrs. Vetch had arranged for in the hotel lobby; and they were then hopping a cab to FAO Schwartz on 5th Avenue a short distance south of the Plaza.

When they arrived at the world-famous toy store, the representatives from Mattel were there as well to discuss product placement and an early promotion just for FAO that showcased the *Mr. Chips!* brand stuffed animals in the most exclusive manner possible.

When they entered the fabulous toy emporium, Jeff could hardly believe his eyes! There, before him, was an Aladdin's castle treasure trove of fancy displays with mounds of every conceivable imported toy, along with board games, doll houses, stuffed animals, model trains and kiddie cars. It was a kid's heaven!

Mr. Chips, however, remained dignified, silent and cool as an underworld spy behind his dark shades. His taciturn demeanor around the dark suits kept them on their back feet as they showed Jeff, Mrs. Vetch and Mr. Chips the prominent location right by the front entrance of the store where the *Mr. Chips!* brand would be initially and exclusively available.

Mr. Chips remained subdued as he looked around the store with the suits dutifully following him and whispering amongst themselves. And as Mr. Chips made a complete circuit around the famous toy palace, he looked through his dark shades at the store's bay window on 5th Avenue, where he saw Red Robin Barnard and Summer Rose, who fluttered their wings and enthusiastically chirped their mutual assent to the placement of Mr. Chips' eponymous stuffed animals up front; whereupon, Mr. Chips at last relented to the hovering suits, barking his unconditional assent, after which Jeff whispered to the suits one final small request from the celebrity canine, the private terms of which were both secret *and* necessary to complete the exclusive *Mr. Chips!* brand business transaction, as outlined by The Vetch family documents and drawn up by their lawyers in consultation with Jeff and Mr. Chips.

****

As Jeff was outlining Mr. Chips' private wish for a special all-electric battery operated and long-distance driving model Rolls Royce Corniche that could travel far and wide on special long-distance batteries, a curtain at the side of the store and directly across from the *Mr. Chips!* brand stuffed animals parted and out came a beautiful young lady guiding the diminutive Rolls Corniche with a remote-control device.

"How'd they do *that?*" Jeff asked.

"When it comes to toys, Mattel can do *anything!*" his mother whispered.

The luxury convertible model toy was complete with a manual drive option and *Mr. Chips'* name specially etched on the driver's side front door. It was moving very slowly and was just the right size for a miniature canine of Mr. Chips' size.

Mesmerized by its style and magical motion, Mr. Chips' eyes lit up when he saw it, then he jumped in, barked and started riding around the whole store on manual override.

"Looks like a dream come true for Mr. Chips!" Jeff said, as Mrs. Vetch smiled at Andy, the Pinkerton guard she had hired, while the men from Mattel and FAO looked on in sheer amazement at the unlikely scene.

"We all knew that man's best friend could be trained; but this little guy should be on Ed Sullivan!" one of the men from FAO Schwartz mentioned.

"Funny you should say that because we're meeting Mr. Sullivan later this week!" Jeff responded.

"Just send the contracts to our lawyers for their review please!" Mrs. Vetch said, "it's just a formality; but I learned from my father Lawrence Wyler to *always* run *all our* business dealings by our lawyers first; after all, my father traveled with his personal attorney!"

"Will do!" the various representatives said as Mr. Chips continued to race around the famous toy emporium in his Lilliputian cream-colored Rolls Corniche with lipstick-red leather seats.

But the *real* surprise of the day was when the men from FAO brought out a miniature model replica of *Sea Cloud,* Marjorie Merriweather Post's famous sailing yacht, for Mr. Chips to enjoy and skipper on the small sailing pond known as Conservatory Waters in Central Park.

Mr. Chips barked his thank you's to all the representatives of FAO and Mattel and a good time was had by all.

CHAPTER THREE: SAILING IN CENTRAL PARK

The next morning, Mr. Chips, Jeff, Mrs. Vetch and Andy, the Pinkerton guard, all headed over to Central Park for a full day of activities, including a planned morning meeting with Bernard Baruch and then a sail on Conservatory Waters including Mr. Chips as captain, Red Robin Barnard as first mate and her baby Summer Rose as second mate.

The Vetch group headed across 59th and walked along 5th Avenue until they had reached 72nd, where they turned west on Terrace Drive and marched along the tree lined route to the miniature sailboat pond, Conservatory Waters, where the esteemed financier Bernard Baruch was sitting as expected at a park bench near the lake; and when he saw the Vetches and Mr. Chips, he smiled and said, "nice to meet you all; now tell me, what investment advice can I offer the Vetch family for their famous canine Mr. Chips?"

"If Jeffrey and Mr. Chips agree, it seems to me that Mr. Chips' upcoming expected income stream from the percentage he'll derive from the sale of his eponymous stuffed animals at Mattel would be wisely directed toward a diversified portfolio of large blue chip common stocks like Coca Cola, Proctor and Gamble, IBM, Colgate Palmolive and Honeywell, to name a few, just to keep it simple and in sync with the way our Vetch family investments are currently managed in Chicago," Mrs. Vetch stated.

"I agree!" Jeff added quickly, "those are the kind of blue-chip stocks that I follow in *The Wall Street Journal,* and I like all of them for the very long haul! But I still don't know how we were able to snag you today for your investment advice, Mr. Baruch!" Jeff added.

"Why that's simple, young man, your mother simply called and asked me, that's all; and, frankly, I didn't have to suggest much of anything because she already had an excellent set of ideas for investment planning which she's laid out here for our consideration this morning, and I, for one, wholeheartedly agree with their premise, not to mention their particulars!" Mr. Baruch mentioned, adding, "I'm sure my friend John Templeton would also agree with such a commonsense investment strategy of developing a diversified portfolio of blue chips for Mr. Chips!" Mr. Baruch concluded.

Meanwhile, Mr. Chips, who had been carrying a miniature brief case on his back, pulled out the latest *New York Times,* turned to the business section and the latest stock columns, looking at the listings on the *NYSE;* and then barked his approval of a broadly diversified blue chip stock portfolio, just as another Pinkerton guard showed up and handed a large container to Andy, the Vetch's personal Pinkerton.

Andy and the other Pinkerton associate then pulled out of the large box an impressive 1/100th scale model of Marjorie Merryweather Post's famous yacht, *Sea Cloud,* which the two guards showed to Mr. Chips, who barked his approval and who scampered over to Conservatory Waters, where the two Pinkertons placed the model electric battery assisted sailing yacht at the water's edge, then Mr. Chip's hopped on board with the help of the two Pinkertons and captained a cruise around the lake that included as special guests, his crew members Red Robin Barnard and her fledgling Summer Rose, who'd just flown over from their ultra luxe potpourri infused pied-a-terre nest at the fabulous French style fin de siecle tower of St. Urban on the upper westside of Central Park.

With Mrs. Vetch, Jeffrey, Mr. Baruch and the two Pinkerton men watching in rapt attention from the shade of the park benches, Mr. Chips and the two robins were granted an unprecedented sailing exemption in being permitted by the Conservatory Waters management to be physically on board their specially outrigged yacht, which was not usually allowed because the rental boats were all remote controlled.

Mr. Chips, Red Robin Barnard and Summer Rose had a wonderful sail in Central Park; while Mr. Baruch, Mrs. Vetch and Jeff confirmed that Mr. Chips' investment strategy would be as simple as trimming one's sails for a successful long term horizon by buying and maintaining a portfolio of broadly diversified American blue chip companies that could be held for an investment lifetime, similar to the way the Vetch family principals were already managed, but tweaked to focus more for long term growth, like those managed for Jeff and his siblings' portfolios.

And after a fabulous sail, a thanks to Mr. Baruch for his agreeable advise confirming Mrs. Vetch's recommendation, then a return of the model yacht to Andy's associate at Pinkerton, who was tasked with shipping it to the family home back in the Midwest, and finally an adieu to Red Robin Barnard and Summer after their mutually enjoyable outing in the park, Mrs. Vetch and Andy, Jeff and Mr. Chips all wandered south through Central Park and back to the corner of 59th and 5th where the Plaza was located.

"What a wonderful day!" Jeff announced as

Mr. Chips barked his approval and Mrs. Vetch said to the Pinkerton guard, "thank you Andy, for all your help today and see you tomorrow!" as the Vetches walked into the 59th Street side entrance by the famous bar of the hotel.

CHAPTER FOUR: MR. CHIPS ON BROADWAY

The next day, Mr. Chips was escorted by the Vetches and Andy, the Pinkerton, to the Mark Hellinger Theater on Broadway in order to interview with the casting director for a one-time walk-on bit-part in the Ascot Opening Race scene of *My Fair Lady,* as a pet on a leash to one of the ladies at the famous event that was showcased in the play.

Of course, Mr. Chips got the part, hands down, or in his case, paws down.

When Jeff and the Pinkerton guard escorted Mr. Chips to the theater several hours before the performance to review his scene, Mr. Chips was completely prepared and wearing the appropriate gray formal-ware and shiny top hat that was featured on some of the men in the scene. And of course, he was silent during his scene and the toast of Broadway that night, as the actors in the play made a big fuss over him before the performance!

With the Vetches in the audience, fifth row center, Mr. Chips nearly stole the show during the famous Ascot Race scene; no easy trick when he shared the stage with the likes of Rex Harrison and Julie Andrews.

That night, Mr. Chips even got to meet Fifi, a dazzlingly beautiful French poodle, who was also in the Ascot scene of the play; but Mr. Chips, always the epitome of discretion, would neither confirm nor deny whether there had been any extracurricular romance or even an assignation between them at the theater that night.

CHAPTER FIVE: BROADWAY & CLUB 21

After his walk-on in *My Fair Lady*, Mr. Chips and Jeff were invited to join Ed Sullivan, the panelists of *What's My Line?* and Topo Gigio for dinner at the back corner table in the lower level of the 21 Club, coincidentally right next to the Vetch family table.

Of course, even with the hysterically funny Topo Gigio in attendance, Mr. Chips stole the show a second time that night, again not an easy thing to do when sitting at a dinner table surrounded by television luminaries Ed Sullivan and his guests including Arlene Francis and Martin Gable as well as Bennett Cerf, Dorothy Kilgallen and their spouses.

"When did you realize that Mr. Chips was extraordinary?" Miss Kilgallen, always the investigative reporter, asked Jeff.

"The moment I saw him dressed to the nines under our Christmas tree, Ma'am!" Jeff responded, as everyone laughed a little, said 'ahhh' and applauded, while the Vetch family at the next table smiled knowingly.

Dinner at 21 Club was a perfect way to conclude another great day in New York City; and by the time the family made it back to the Plaza, they and Mr. Chips were uniformly tuckered out and ready for a good night's sleep.

CHAPTER SIX: TIMES SQUARE

Mr. Chips and Jeff decided the very next morning that no trip to New York City was complete without visiting Times Square and the Empire State Building. When they arrived at the iconic midtown skyscraper with their security guard Andy, Mr. Chips barked that they must take the elevator up to the viewing observatory near the top. When they arrived, Mr. Chips barked his insistence that he be lifted up to see the panoramic scene of Manhattan; and no sooner had Jeff held him up to enjoy the view, then Mr. Chips stated to bark, as if to alert his friends all over the vast metropolis that he had arrived.

And suddenly, Manhattan was filled with the sounds of pooches barking all over the island, as if in unison. What a cacophony of racket it was that wafted clear up to the rarified air of the Empire State Building's observatory!

By the time that Jeff and Andy had escorted Mr. Chips from the skyscraper to Times Square, a mob of puppies and their owners were there and crowding around Nathan's Famous hotdog emporium, where Mr. Chips and all his newfound New York City friends enjoyed a hit treat and their very own hot diggity hotdog, each one, courtesy of the folks at Nathan's Famous. And all the newspapers and magazine reporters were there to showcase the madhouse canine scene on the local evening news on WABC, WCBS and WNBC! The place looked like a set for a Disney film location!

By the time Jeff and Mr. Chips returned to the family suite at the Plaza, everyone was huddled around the television, watching the taped broadcast of Mr. Chips and his canine pals earlier in the day swamping the stalled traffic at Times Square while scarfing down their hot diggity hotdogs! A good time was had by all that day in the heart of midtown Manhattan, thanks to Mr. Chips and his best friend and pal Jeff!

CHAPTER SEVEN: MATTEL & INVESTMENTS

The following morning, Mr. Chips, accompanied by Jeff and the Pinkerton guard, strolled down 5th Avenue to the legendary toy store FAO Schwartz once more, in order to check out Mr. Chips' eponymous stuffed animal line. What they could *not* have expected was a display of the Mr. Chips stuffed animals already showcased in the FAO window facing 5th Avenue; and when Mr. Chips insisted on barking his approval while scampering into the display window and running all around it, passersby stopped to see what all the fuss was about; and a madhouse scene of adult customers and their children stampeded into the store to purchase the initial display of *Mr. Chips!* brand stuffed animals in the storefront window.

After a near panic and rush of people crowded into the store, their corporate security had to block further entry, while Jeff and Andy, the Pinkerton guard, safely whisked Mr. Chips into the back employee storage rooms, where coincidentally Mr. Chips was able to see his Rolls Royce Corniche car which FAO was personalizing just for him. He barked his approval after checking out the special outfitting of his new Rolls Corniche; after which he, Jeff and Andy were driven home to the Plaza in one of FAO's special unmarked vans with dark tinted windows, thus escaping unnoticed the crush of fans that were still swarming around the front entry as well as the cashier's desk toward the back of the famous toy store.

"Keep your heads down!" Andy said to Jeff and Mr. Chips, as the company van pulled out of the alley contiguous to the store and onto 5th Avenue, where crowds were milling about near the entrance to FAO Schwartz.

They had miraculously made the turn onto the busy thoroughfare without being blocked or noticed and then disappeared north on 5th Avenue toward the Plaza before any of the throng mobbing the toy store realized they had escaped! It had been a great success of a day for Mr. Chips and Jeff. Their clever anonymity in departing worked like a charm!

CHAPTER EIGHT: CONEY ISLAND

Mr. Chips and Jeff, accompanied by their Pinkerton guard, spent the following day at Coney Island, where they all got to enjoy another delicious hot diggity dog at the park's very own Nathan's Famous, after which they walked around the iconic setting.

When they approached the old wooden roller coaster, *The Cyclone,* Mr. Chips let out a bark of insistence that was clear enough to Jeff.

"It's pretty obvious he wants to ride!" Andy said.

"He's too small!" responded Jeff; "but let's see what the operator says!"

Mr. Chips barked his approval of the plan; and, surprisingly, when they walked up to the roller coaster operator, he signed off on Mr. Chips going on the ride as long as Jeff held onto him while they were both strapped into the seat harness and protective gear.

After they buckled up and the roller coaster took off and climbed the steep rise to the top, Mr. Chips let out a yip and bark, threw up his front paws, mimicking Jeff and the riders in front of them; and then the coaster began to slowly roll over the crest of the tracks before plunging at a forty-five-degree angle to the bottom.

Mr. Chips barked all the way down the hill and then back up, as the roller coaster made its way on the ancient creaky tracks and around the wooden trestles of the wavy configuration; and when they arrived at the end of the ride, Jeff let out a 'yay', Mr. Chips signaled his approval with a single bark, and Andy guided them to a nearby bench where they could take a breather after all that excitement!

Coney Island was fun for Jeff and Mr. Chips because they were able to enjoy themselves without being noticed; and they were also safe because of the Pinkerton guard, who never let them out of his sight while he was on duty.

A great day was had by all at Coney Island, most especially for Mr. Chips!

CHAPTER NINE:
FIFTH AVENUE

The next day, Jeff was determined to take Mr. Chips ice skating at Rockefeller Center; and as soon as Andy arrived for his morning shift, Jeff asked Mr. Chips if he wanted an adventure on the ice.

Mr. Chips barked in the affirmative; and the three of them took off down 5th Avenue for a fun time on the rink.

When they arrived at the famous ice-skating venue, the joint was jumping. Mr. Chips, always prepared, opened up his knapsack which he'd been carrying on his back, and then he pulled out four sapphire colored ice skates, barked for Jeff's assistance in strapping them on; and, lo and behold, he was ready for his star turn on the ice!

With Jeff and the Pinkerton guard casually skating on the perimeter and keeping a watch on him, Mr. Chips showed off the breadth of his skill at ice skating by his many adeptly performed jumps, spins and turns around the rink.

Everybody on the rink was mesmerized by Mr. Chips' elegant performance; and, by the end of their all to brief time at Rockefeller Center, Mr. Chips had made a whole new group of friends.

CHAPTER TEN: WALL STREET

After Mr. Chips and Jeff returned to FAO Schwartz the next day, the store manager presented Mr. Chips with an advance on his eponymous doll sales, after which Mr. Chips barked a request of Jeff to take him to his brokers at Goldman Sachs, where he bought stock in several blue chips, including the ones that had been reviewed earlier in Central Park with Mrs. Vetch and Mr. Baruch.

The team at Goldman Sachs were very helpful; and Mr. Chips was on his way to financial independence, with the beginnings of a broadly diversified portfolio of blue-chip common stocks. Mr. Chips already knew the answer to the question that day:— namely, 'who *doesn't* love common stock shares in Coca Cola, Proctor and Gamble and Colgate Palmolive?'

CHAPTER ELEVEN: MR. CHIPS GOES SNOWBOARDING AT VAN CORTLANDT PARK

On the last day of the trip, Mr. Chips barked his insistence on going snowboarding and cross-country skiing; and, of course, that meant only one place in the city, — why, Van Cortlandt Park, naturally.

They borrowed the rented family limousine, and with the help of the chauffeur Mr. Thomas, were driven over to the Bronx and the thousand-acre park, where Jeff, Andy and Mr. Chips donned their rented cross-country skis and had a blast enjoying their last day in the city in the perfect snowfall of a perfect winter day!

"Mr. Chips, does a trip to New York City end better than this?" Jeff asked him as they flew down the hill together.

Mr. Chips' gleeful barks said it all as he charged ahead and left Jeff in the dust!

CHAPTER TWELVE: IDLEWILD FIRST CLASS HOME

Mr. Chips, by now a famous celebrity puppy, got to jet home a big success after taking New York City by storm and flying as a pampered pooch on Pan Am first class with Jeff next to him, while the rest of the family humorously pretended to sulk just behind them in bulkhead coach.

"Now that he's gonna be rich and is already famous, Mr. Chips won't need us anymore!" Mrs. Vetch said to Dr. Vetch.

"I'm not quite sure that's completely true, Mother!" Alec wisely observed.

"We *all* need you, Mother!" Sharon added, echoing Alec's sentiment.

And of course that *was true!*

****

From behind the bulkhead wall of the plane, the family could hear that Mr. Chips let out a bark of agreement with Sharon's heartfelt sentiment; and Jeff got up out of his seat in first class next to Mr. Chips and came through the curtain divider to coach class, announcing, "Mr. Chips is one of us, so there are no concerns because he *is* a Vetch *after all!*

And that, folks, says it all!

BOOK V: MISTER CHIPS ON THE COTE D'AZUR

CHAPTER ONE: MR. CHIPS AT THE CARLTON HOTEL IN CANNES

Summer 1960

After a perfectly wonderful cross-Atlantic jet flight and then a lovely late morning sleep, Mr. Chips stretched his little legs and woke up after midday in his hotel suite, a well-rested pooch in his miniature mauve satin pillowed bed. The bright golden rays of sunshine poured through the opened patio doors, where Mr. Chips looked out at the Mediterranean and saw Lilliputian sailboats floating lazily by the famed hotel. The scene was as charming as only the French Riviera could be!

Mr. Chips stood up in his satin pajamas, shook himself awake and scampered over to the patio, where he could view the entire panorama of Cannes' magnificent coastline, which stretched along La Croisette, the famous waterfront thoroughfare, in both directions.

Mr. Chips then surveyed the beach on each side of the hotel; and he saw a vast sparkling necklace of palm trees fluttering in the wind along the waterfront thoroughfare. Why, the scene of Cannes' waterfront appeared like one of those big splashy paintings of Bernard Buffet that hung in the Vetch's dining room! There were beautiful second empire mansard roofed buildings of modest height that were harmoniously situated along the Mediterranean in the most picturesque manner. Cannes France gleamed in the shimmering morning light!

Mr. Chips wagged his tail as he looked at the pedestrians and traffic passing in front of the Carlton Hotel, where he was on vacation with his family, the Vetches from Glencoe. They were all on a European summer holiday in June of the year 1960 and Mr. Chips was happy to be included!

****

Jeff, the ten-year-old boy who took care of him and was Mr. Chips' best buddy, also woke up to his little friend and German schnauzer nuzzling him; and said, "what a beautiful day it is for the beach, darling Mr. Chips!"

Mr. Chips barked enthusiastically and scurried over to his bed; but he had other fun ideas on his mind that morning as he scampered back over to the patio and looked down along La Croisette and stared at the crowds of goofy pedestrians and the crazy quilt of traffic, beyond which Mr. Chips focused on the sparkling sand, where the limitless multicolored umbrellas stretched along the famed Riviera beach in both directions all the way to the horizon.

In the bright sunshine of the morning, Mr. Chips could see the palm trees fluttering along the shoreline which framed the Cote D'Azur, and beyond which were a scattering of impressive luxury yachts and sailing schooners, the largest of which was *Seacloud*, Marjorie Merriweather Post's massive white sailboat, reigning supreme on the glittering blue waters in the center of the crescent shaped bay, like a sparkling diamond jewel in a sapphire crown. Mr. Chips remembered the model of *Seacloud* he'd skippered around Conservatory Waters in New York City that past Christmas vacation; and now he marveled at the impressive ship sitting out in the Mediterranean in front of the Carlton Hotel; and because of its distance from the shoreline, it appeared no larger than the scale model, a trick of perspective.

When next Mr. Chips looked directly left and east, he could see all the way to Cap Ferat and the Hotel Du Cap; while at the summit of the cliffs behind the hotel, Mr. Chips turned, craned his little neck and looked way up high to the very location of the vertiginous and twisty route of the Grande Corniche, where he wanted to explore the terrain by himself and in his very own specially made miniature Rolls Corniche convertible.

****

While Mr. Chips was contemplating his plans for the day, Jeff picked up the local newspaper, the latest edition of *Nice-Matin* that had been slipped by a valet under the hotel room door; and proclaimed, "look, Mr. Chips, the Duke and Duchess of Windsor will be on Madame Post's yacht *Seacloud* along with Princess Grace today and throughout the week! That means they're likely sailing in the harbor right out in front of our hotel now!" Jeff announced excitedly, "so let's go down to the harbor right away and check it all out!" he added.

Mr. Chips first looked at Jeff with a wondrous expression, then scampered back over to the opened windows and the French doors to stare out at the magnificent sailing yacht owned by Mrs. Post; and finally, he wagged his tail in sheer astonishment at the beautiful Mediterranean Sea of the Cote D'Azur sparkling in the morning sunshine. Then Mr. Chips barked his full agreement with Jeff's plan.

CHAPTER TWO: MR. CHIPS' FABULOUS ROLLS CORNICHE

After Jeff had showered and dressed elegantly for a stroll along La Croisette with his canine ward, he then helped Mr. Chips into an appropriate outfit for promenading along the famous avenue; and they each let Mrs. Vetch know in their own unique style that they were heading downstairs for a little fun in the sun. And, with the aforementioned proclamation from Jeff and a coincidental bark from Mr. Chips, the two best buddies were on their way to the waterfront and La Croisette!

As the front door to the hotel suite was closing behind him, Jeff heard his mother's stentorian voice, "do not stray far from the grounds of the Carlton Hotel, Jeffrey Joseph! I don't want to spend the whole day looking for you!" Mrs. Vetch admonished her youngest son, who knew that, whenever she used his middle name, she was *very serious*. Jeff innately understood that being deferential to his mother was always smart.

Jeff found it immensely enjoyable that he had a gorgeous hotel room with an amazing view; but he certainly didn't want to be cooped up in it all day while there was other fun to be had in the sunny south of France; right there along the promenade of the French Riviera!

Looking over at his pooch in the hotel corridor, he asked Mr. Chips, "you wanna have some fun today?"

Mr. Chips displayed his enthusiasm by wagging his diminutive tail and barking loudly in the affirmative.

"Let's go back to the room then and check out your model automobile!" Jeff said to Mr. Chips, who followed him back into their hotel suite and looked over at the box containing his miniature touring Rolls Royce, which Jeff removed from its special velvet lined suitcase and carefully protected wrapping paper, and then placed on the floor for Mr. Chips to test drive in the hotel room.

Mr. Chips beamed and barked as he scampered over to it and drove the little convertible *all* around the suite. It was a very small version of the perfectly designed touring car, tailored exactly to fit his diminutive use; while it also possessed an all-day battery charge that was crafted especially for long distance driving, though Jeff had no idea *why* Mr. Chips could *possibly* need such a battery feature.

After Mr. Chips took a test run around the hotel suite, Jeff placed the model automobile in its special dome-shaped carrier with its handy leather handle for ease of use, then zipped it up safely and said to Mr. Chips, "allons-y!" It was time to once again head downstairs and see the fabulous city of Cannes and all its delightful waterfront sights.

"Stay close to me at all times when we're on La Croisette!" Jeff ordered Mr. Chips, who barked his seeming acquiescence, "and wear your disguise because you're very popular here in France and your stuffed animals are being sold *everywhere, even* in the hotel lobby gift shop, where the staff in the entry know you're staying here!" Jeff added.

At ten years old, Jeff was not worried in the slightest. What could possibly go wrong with this simple plan of fun in the sun, carrying the Rolls in the miniature suitcase and with Mr. Chips in disguise, in Cannes no less; and in broad daylight on one of the most famous beachfront boulevards in the world?

Why, nothing of course, Jeff thought to himself, as he looked at Mr. Chips, who had donned an outfit that made him look like a cold war spy, featuring a dark trench coat and midnight shades. After Mr. Chips was accoutered and in disguise, they took the elevator down to the main lobby floor, where they tiptoed quietly and sideways behind an obscuring line of tall potted palm tree plants along the back lobby wall so as not to be seen by the hotel guests in the entry loggia.

The two of them had miraculously made it undetected through the cavernous room of the hotel lobby and past the front desk where a panoply of the *Mr. Chips!* brand dolls were displayed. At last, they made it to the outside front entrance of the hotel, then on toward the bustling boulevard, where Mr. Chips wagged his tail and barked to Jeff to please cross the street with him at the pedestrian walk, so as to be on the seaside of the crazily busy thoroughfare.

Upon doing so, Mr. Chips then barked to Jeff to please take the Rolls out of the travel bag, 'merci beaucoup', which Jeff, unthinking, did, whereupon Mr. Chips jumped in, turned on the battery-operated ignition and took off so fast down the sidewalk that Jeff didn't even have time to shout, "Arrêt! this instant, Mr. Chips!"

And just like that, in that very instant, Mr. Chips and the Rolls were gone! They had disappeared along the seaside pedestrian sidewalk of La Croisette!

When Jeff last saw him, Mr. Chips was giggling in merriment and going like gangbusters, driving his miniature Rolls at top speed along La

Croisette with his goggles and his cold war spy trench coat on, a red silk *Hermes* scarf blowing behind him in the wind and a French navy beret firmly attached to his head.

South along La Croisette, past many tourist gift shops displaying *Mr. Chips!* brand toy puppies, Mr. Chips drove his model car at such a breakneck speed that he was merely observed as a blur by the crush of onlookers he rushed by, weaving through them like an invisible snake through underbrush in a mad dash for canine freedom.

Onward Mr. Chips charged, speeding headlong south on the sidewalk of La Croisette, expertly driving his Lilliputian vehicle through the throngs of pedestrians on the busy seaside thoroughfare. He flew by the tourist crowds along the waterfront in a crazy cloud of dust, then turned north on Rue La Tour to Avenue Windsor and on up the steep incline of the hill toward the corniches and the highest of the three cliffside roads, the hairpin turns of the spectacular Grand Corniche, a perfect road for a Hitchcock thriller, where, upon reaching the circuitous route, he pulled over to the Mediterranean side of the road overlooking the Cote D'Azur, parked, pulled out his pocket set of binoculars; and, focusing on *Seacloud,* the legendary sailing yacht, Mr. Chips expertly espied Marjorie Merriweather Post enjoying a steaming hot beverage with Princess Grace and Their Royal Highnesses, The Duke and Duchess of

Windsor.

And in that very instant, Mr. Chips knew that *that was* one yacht party whose eminences he wanted to join; but *only* after he had visited a couple of the French Riviera's most alluring destinations.

CHAPTER THREE: MR. CHIPS GAMBLES BIG AT THE FAMED CASINO IN MONACO

With thoughts of that royal shipboard party dancing in his head, Mr. Chips proceeded to drive his little Rolls Corniche all the way back down each of the three Corniches and right to the very spot where his best friend and confidante, Jeff Vetch, his diminutive and young boss, was patiently waiting for him, transfixed and scratching his head with a look of complete puzzlement on his furrowed brow.

"Where on God's green earth have you been, young fellow? I was looking all about for you; and I was really quite worried about you!" Jeff stated; as an unrepentant Mr. Chips looked longingly up the hill to the Grand Corniche, where he'd just been. How lovely an afternoon it had been for him, driving in his miniature Corniche on *the Grande Corniche!*

"Ok, Mr. Chips, I get it! You just wanted a little 'alone' time, a little 'me' time, isn't that correct, Mr. Chips?" Jeff asked humorously.

Mr. Chips barked in the affirmative.

"How'd you like to go to the Casino in Monaco tonight?" Jeff asked his buddy.

Once again, Mr. Chips barked in the affirmative.

When they arrived back in their hotel suite, Jeff asked Mrs. Vetch if the entire family, including Mr. Chips, might be able to go to the Monaco Casino that evening; and surprisingly, after checking with Dr. Vetch, she agreed to take them all, including his siblings Alec and Sharon, to the Casino.

After a quick shower and a spritz of Aqua Velva, Jeff helped Mr. Chips don his black tux and shiny black Gucci shoes, after which Mr. Chips put on his dark Ray-Ban shades and top hat, then grabbed his glittering diamond colored rhinestone walking stick; and he was all ready for a fun night out at the iconic roulette table in Monaco's famous Casino.

When the Vetches arrived at the Casino, the family was mobbed by onlookers and autograph seekers who wanted to get a glimpse of the two famous buddies from the moment Jeff and Mr. Chips stepped out of the Vetch's chauffeur driven limousine in their matching tuxes, shades and glittering walking sticks.

Straight to the roulette table Mr. Chips went, with the Vetch entourage following Jeff and him. When Jeff and Mr. Chips arrived at the storied salon, Princess Grace happened to be in attendance, along with luminaries including Sean Connery and Sir Ian Fleming.

"I thought that you were never *ever* in the casino, Your Grace; and that you *were* on Mrs. Post's yacht today!" Jeff said unabashedly, after introducing himself and Mr. Chips, who bowed gracefully to her and then did a little gavotte for effect.

Ignoring his former observation, the princess responded to the latter by saying, "Mrs. Post gave me the night off for good behavior, though I *am* spending the week on her sailboat with her special guests!" the Princess of Monaco responded tactfully, continuing, "Mrs. Post showed me the *Mr. Chips!* stuffed animal she'd acquired; and I thought it was so cute, I only hope that you both can join us day after tomorrow, if you're available for high tea on board!" the princess said, handing Jeff two small specially engraved guest cards for exclusive entry to the legendary yacht on the specified day.

"Incredible place!" marveled Alec, as he looked around the interior of the casino.

Staring at Mr. Connery, Sharon asked, "Is that whom I think he is?"

"Yes, no doubt!" Dr. Vetch answered.

Jeff placed a large number of high value chips on the roulette table on behalf of Mr. Chips, then bet on the number of times Mr. Chips had barked, seven, which serendipitously hit. Mr. Chips, having won big, was done for the evening after a single large bet and then hightailed it, walking away from the casino roulette salon a substantial winner, further cementing his mystique as a savvy hirsute success story, a canine whiz of a kid!

What a night it was for the Vetches and their extraordinary Mr. Chips! He had marched into the joint a famous guy; and when he walked out with a nice chunk of the iconic casino's money, Mr. Chips was a good deal richer. Mr. Chips innately understood that, while fame is great, wealth is better, and cash is *always* king!

CHAPTER FOUR:
MR. CHIPS AT
THE GLAMOROUS
HOTEL DU CAP
IN CAP FERAT

T he next morning, Jeff asked his brother and sister to drive him and Mr. Chips to the Hotel Du Cap for lunch; and he was pleasantly surprised when they both agreed to accompany the two of them in the family rental car. The drive to the famous resort, located in between Cannes and Monaco on the Cote D'Azur, was stunningly beautiful; and they marveled at the scenery along the famous route.

After a gorgeous ride along the storied coastline that had attracted the rich and famous for centuries, they arrived at the famed hotel, where they dropped the vehicle off with the valets and then entered the magnificent lobby, the seaside view from which was captivating and charming.

As they walked through the lobby and by the hotel gift shop, there on display were *Mr. Chips!* brand stuffed animals, which delighted their canine companion's inspiration. Mr. Chips wagged his tail and barked when he saw his little eponymous likenesses upon the gift shop sales counter.

Dressed nattily in sartorial splendor with a pink lapel rose on his rare gray seersucker suit, the pattern of which blended with his pewter colored hair, Mr. Chips also wore miniature Gucci shoes and had on a straw sun hat with a pink sash tied in a bow around its top while Jeff, Sharon and Alec were all dressed nicely in breezy, casually elegant resort cruise wear.

When they entered the hotel dining room, Mr. Chips was stunned and wagged his tail when he saw the Duke and Duchess of Windsor, who last were seen by him through his binoculars on the famous yacht *Seacloud,* parked right out in front of the Carlton Hotel in Cannes two days earlier.

Remarkably, Jeff, his siblings and Mr. Chips were seated right next to the famous English royal couple, who, upon noticing the Vetches and recognizing their famous canine companion, jointly said, "good day, Mr. Chips!" to the famous puppy, whose breeding taught him to maintain his composure in such a rarified setting, bowing but absolutely *not* barking in the presence of such lofty personages.

"You must join us tomorrow on *Seacloud* if you can!" the Duchess of Windsor affirmed, uncharacteristically gushing, "Mrs. Post is just *dying* to meet you!"

"Thank you, thank you, I will see to it that Mr. Chips is on time tomorrow for high tea, to which Princess Grace has already invited us yesterday!" Jeff said disarmingly.

"How charming!" the Duke of Windsor responded.

Alec and Sharon were stunned by the ease of familiarity between their younger brother and these famous royals; and they garnered new respect for Jeff, despite his extraordinarily young age. They couldn't imagine how their kid brother could be comfortable with such lofty personages, considering that they still thought of Jeff as their own little *Dennis the Menace!*

****

The three Vetch siblings and their companion, Mr. Chips, enjoyed a delicious lunch of Salad Niçoise and Crab Louie, Provençal style, at the world famous hotel; then, after saying their polite adieus to the Duke and Duchess of Windsor, they walked around the celebrated resort grounds and marveled at the romantically beautiful views of the Mediterranean, finally departing for their return journey to Cannes along the seaside after an unforgettable meal and unexpected chance meeting at the Hotel Du Cap with one of the most famous royal couples in the world.

CHAPTER FIVE:
MR. CHIPS SAILS
WITH THE DUKE
AND DUCHESS
OF WINDSOR

The very next morning, the phone rang at eleven, Dr. Vetch picked up the receiver and said, "please hold a moment", then called to Mrs. Vetch, using her nickname, "Doe, it's Mrs. Post's secretary, confirming with you that you are permitting your son Jeffrey and his ward, Mr. Chips, to join her, Princess Grace and the Duke and Duchess of Windsor on *Seacloud;* and she mentioned that Mrs. Post instructed her to inform us to please join them on the yacht today if we're also available!" Dr. Vetch concluded.

"Of course we would have loved to attend! Please tell Mrs. Post's secretary that we send our regrets, as we already have plans with our friends, the ambassador and his wife, at the Hotel Du Cap this afternoon; but we'll see to it that Jeffrey and Mr. Chips are ferried out!" Mrs. Vetch responded.

"Will do!" the doctor answered.

"Get a time they need to be there, Ade!" Mrs. Vetch said, using his nickname.

"Ok, yes," Mrs. Vetch heard Dr. Vetch say into the receiver, "yes, uh, huh, yeah, got it, yep, two pm, yes, ok, thank you, ma'am, yep, uh huh, ok, Joan, thank you and we'll see to it that they're there out there at two pm properly accoutered to meet their Royal Highnesses, the Duke and Duchess of Windsor, yes ma'am, and regards to Mrs. Post, of course!" Dr. Vetch said respectfully, then hung up the phone receiver, saying, "whew, *that* was assuredly *something*!" he added, then called out to Jeff, "make sure you both are dressed appropriately by noon for your venerable hostess and I'll make reservations at the front desk with the guest concierge to valet you by courtesy shuttle from the hotel entrance to the harbor ferry which will then transfer you and Mr. Chips out to *Seacloud* at one pm so that you two are assured of arriving onboard Mrs. Post's yacht by the designated time of two pm."

Mr. Chips let out a bark of excitement; and Jeff made sure they were both properly accoutered in matching dark navy blue Pucci suits and pink Charvet ties with pale blue pocket squares, Ferragamo black leather shoes, dark Ray-Ban shades and a spritz of classic Old Spice cologne for freshness and fun.

By the time they were dressed and ready, Dr. Vetch stated matter-of-factly to Jeff, "if you and Mr. Chips are all set to go to the concierge downstairs, your older brother and sister will escort you both to the lobby!"

Alec and Sharon waited patiently until Dr. and Mrs. Vetch had been treated to a show of snazzy elegance, preserved for posterity courtesy of Sharon and her Polaroid Instamatic.

Nattily dressed Mr. Chips and his handsome caretaker, Jeff, posed for pictures in their hotel suite; images that were enhanced by the reflections from the living room's backdrop of antique French mirrors, adding just a touch of glamor and ambience to the photographic tableau. Sharon wanted to be a renowned photographer one day and her iconic images at the Carlton Hotel were a great beginning.

"Have fun dear and use your best manners!" Mrs. Vetch mentioned to her young quiescent son as Mr. Chips let out a single bark of good-natured agreement. Jeff was primped, cherubic and dazzling in his shimmering Pucci and finally ready, calling out his goodbye to his mother, while Mr. Chips was tapping his Ferragamos in the ironic humor of feigned impatience until the moment had arrived; and away the three siblings went, with Alec and Sharon escorting their kid brother and his canine ward down to the concierge desk for their superstars, the venerable Mr. Chips', and Jeff's departure on their special seaborne adventure along the Cote D'Azur.

****

A short while later, Jeff and Mr. Chips were being ferried out to the magnificent sailing yacht, *Seacloud,* which was more impressive up close than at a distance, because of the sheer immensity of its size.

As their ferry came up close enough to the yacht to disembark, Jeff said, "wha'd'ya think of *that*, Mr. Chips?"

Mr. Chips let out a cute little polite bark of agreement, which caused the Duchess of Windsor to look over the side and proclaim, "the two guests of honor are here!" the irony of the comment that *anyone other than her* would be a guest of honor in that setting, completely lost on the young and inexperienced Master Jeffrey and his fancy Monsieur Chips, neither of whom were familiar with being in the company of such exalted eminences!

"Nice to meet you, Mrs. Post!" Jeff said to his

hostess, who proceeded to introduce him and Mr. Chips to the Duke and Duchess of Windsor as well as the Princess of Monaco.

"We've already met at the casino!" the princess intoned, as the Duchess added, "as have we, darlings!"

Mr. Chips was on his very best behavior that afternoon enjoying cake and high tea; and he was the very epitome of decorum and dignity throughout the sail, avoiding either running around the decks or letting out with even a *single* bark. Without even trying, Mr. Chips was a born 'natural', once again stealing the show; and by the time the elegant sail had come to an end, Jeff and his canine companion had won the hearts of both their extraordinary hostess and her exalted royal guests, thanks to the cutest schnauzer in the whole world, the effervescent and indomitable Mr. Chips!

CHAPTER SIX: MR. CHIPS HANGS OUT AT DA BOUTTAU

Within a decent scamper of the Carlton Hotel was the legendary Da Bouttau Auberge, to which Mr. Chips barked his approval, when Jeff mentioned possibly visiting it together with him. Picasso was known to frequent the legendary place; and Mr. Chips had wanted to meet the famous artist ever since Jeff had brought home the ceramic designed artwork which he had constructed in lapidary class of a scene featuring a highly embellished and stylized interpretation of the famous artist's magnificent chateau in the south of France.

"They have beef ribs for you and bouillabaisse for me at Da Bouttau, Mr. Chips; wha'dja'think of that?" Jeff asked.

After Mr. Chips barked his enthusiastic agreement, Jeff sought Mrs. Vetch's approval, which she remarkably granted him; and they were immediately off for a fun lunch with Alec and Sharon as chaperones.

A half hour later and after a pretty good hike along La Croisette, Jeff, his siblings and Mr. Chips found the famous restaurant, where they were surprised to see both the famous painter and Sean Connery dining; and when the four of them walked in together, everyone in the restaurant turned to see them. The patrons of the establishment knew who Mr. Chips and his caretakers were because his escapades along the Cote D'Azur had just been seen on local television and written up in the local newspapers, including their recent sail on Mrs. Post's *Seacloud.*

Mr. Chips was quite a sight to behold that day, all decked out like a famous painter, with just the right sort of quirky artist smock outfit on, a paintbrush in his lapel pocket, a navy French chapeau tilted at just the perfectly exquisite angle for that certain air of 'je ne sis quoi'; and, completing the look, midnight Ray-Ban shades obscuring his eyes.

After being petted by several of the restaurant's patrons, Mr. Chips returned to the Vetch table and the meal which Jeff had ordered for him, a steaming delicious bowl of beef ribs which Mr. Chips could languorously munch on, while Jeff enjoyed the signature dish of fabulous bouillabaisse that Da Bouttau was famous for.

And, to cap off the day's entertainment, a fine time was had by all there who were treated to the delightful rhapsodies of a trio of handsomely accoutered minstrels playing a wonderful selection of classic French tunes.

And once again, the adorable Mr. Chips was as charming as the setting of the world famous Da Bouttau restaurant; and, to top it off, Mr. Chips considerately didn't utter a single bark, not even when Picasso handed him a pencil drawing of his likeness on a restaurant paper napkin!

CHAPTER SEVEN: MR. CHIPS AND THE RED FOX

The highlight of the next day was the chauffeur driven evening ride into the hills above Cannes and Nice, courtesy of the driver, whose family had a charmingly secluded restaurant that was known for its spectacular Baked Alaska and Napoleon slices for dessert.

"Are we going to *La Reine Pédauque?*" Jeff asked.

"No, we are not! You'll just have to be surprised!" Dr. Vetch said, though he knew that it would be a splendid dinner at another one of the Riviera's many wonderful restaurants: — this one, a hidden gem, courtesy of their chauffeur's family.

After they drove up the hill to the lowest of the corniches, they wound their way through the spectacular scenery that included dazzling views of the Mediterranean in between wooded areas and precipitous cliffs, finally arriving at the private location, where they were greeted by the chauffeur's family, owners of the establishment, and were quickly seated.

After the Vetch's perused the menu and decided upon letting the restauranteur family prepare their 'specialties de la Maison', it became clear that the unique 'specialty' which caught Mr. Chips attention was also the very same one that the restaurant's fiery mascot and pet red fox, Henri, *also* wished on that particular night, the one and *only* available portion of the classic dish of osso bucco. Mr. Chips had no choice but to insist on a symbolic dueling sword match with the fox, to be held in the restaurant's back kitchen garden, with the winner getting to enjoy the specially prepared signature dish of osso bucco.

Henri, the red fox, graciously accepted Mr. Chips' challenge of a friendly, fair and safe sword match for a chance to win the meal, with each of the principals choosing a second; which, in Mr. Chips' case, was Jeff, of course, while on Henri's, it was the establishment's sommelier. Helmets were required and the combatants' swords were specially round and rubber tipped for safety precautions and to avoid any risk of injury.

While Dr. and Mrs. Vetch and Jeff's older brother and sister ignored the cartoonish combat out back, the theatrical duel proceeded. The Vetch family pretended to be oblivious to the hirsute nonsense masquerading as noblesse oblige in the backyard; and instead, dined inside the private family operated establishment on a fine meal including a gorgeous Chardonnay served with an appetizer of escargot, a Caesar salad, and then a Bordeaux joined with an entrée of Chateaubriand, petite vegetables with potatoes au gratin, followed by coffee and a choice of freshly created Baked Alaska or Napoleon slices for dessert.

The Vetches were too busy enjoying their delightful meal to pay attention to the bright lights of the well-fenced kitchen garden, a perfectly private setting for Mr. Chips' contrived duel.

The seemingly unconcerned family knew that Mr. Chips and his guardian were going to do whatever they pleased in any case, so Mrs. Vetch had simply instructed Jeff to be ready with Mr. Chips to depart the restaurant for the limousine ride back down the corniche to their Riviera hotel when the family had finished their unforgettable meal, undisturbed by the histrionic schadenfreude outside!

"What *exactly were* you two doing out back while we were dining inside?" Mrs. Vetch asked her young son in the parking lot, as he and Mr. Chips came around the corner of the house all puffed up by their victory over the red fox and his 'second'.

"We were engaged in a jousting match

with Henri, the house red fox and his second, the restaurant's sommelier!" Jeff responded accurately, as if such a thing wasn't unusual in the slightest.

Hearing what her young son announced, but not paying any *real* attention to what it was he had actually *said,* his mother simply responded, "that's nice dear; I hope you and brave Mr. Chips enjoyed yourselves and had as wonderful a time as we did!"

"We sure did!" Jeff said, as Mr. Chips barked in agreement.

"Did Mr. Chips come out on top?" Alec whispered to his younger brother.

"He *always does!*" Jeff answered, as he smiled at Mr. Chips, who'd won the red fox's navy-blue beret, fair and square, as well as a victory meal of osso bucco with a garnish of asparagus, along with petite portions of garlic whipped potatoes and baby carrots; not a bad showing for a glamorous canine!

It was another adventurous night out on the town for the dashing Mr. Chips in the charmingly bucolic setting of that private family restaurant high in the hills above Cannes, completely unmarked on the corniche and where the Vetch family dined in elegance at one of the Cote D'Azur's most hidden and alluring gastronomic establishments whose very name was never revealed.

Some private experiences in life are so special that they are best kept that way. Outside of the Vetches, only Mr. Chips knew of the restaurant's true identity, and he never gave it away.

CHAPTER EIGHT: MR. CHIPS WATER- SKIS ON THE COTE D'AZUR

Nobody in the Vetch family other than Jeff expected to see Mr. Chips *ever water-ski;* but Jeff knew that his furry friend could do just about *anything* he set his mind to, and waterskiing was *one* such thing!

Just to prove the point, Jeff had had four specially designed miniature canine skis fabricated for a puppy of Mr. Chips' exact size, weight and paw size. Then Jeff arranged for Mr. Chips to receive the finest instruction available, right there on the Cote D'Azur; and from an English-speaking animal trainer with expertise in canine acrobatics, to boot!

Jeff wanted to show the throngs of tourists along the Riviera waterfront exactly *what* his canine buddy could do on the calm waters of the Mediterranean! Mr. Chips had been given specially fabricated miniature air-filled skis attached to each other across and front to back and carefully constructed so that his four paws could be inserted into them. He would then be pulled along in the water on these floating skis behind a remote-controlled Lilliputian model toy motorboat, a scale model of Mrs. Dodge's fabulous yacht, *Delphine,* specially designed for Mr. Chips' modest proportions.

A bespoke harness was built to go around Mr. Chips midriff and the rope was attached underneath and from his stomach, stretching all the way to the boat ten feet in front of him, so that, when Jeff called out, "ready, Mr. Chips!" and the puppy nodded affirmatively, Jeff put the little model boat in forward gear and off Mr. Chips went along the waterfront, causing another sensation on La Croisette that day and featured on the late news that very night!

After Mr. Chips completed the brief water-ski adventure in front of the Carlton Hotel, Jeff directed the miniature motor craft to the beach where he was standing; and Mr. Chips was untied from his harness and floating skis to thunderous applause from the onlooking crowd.

"I know you want to go back out water-skiing again!" Jeff said to his canine ward, who had stars in his eyes, "and I promise you that you will someday; but let's call it a success here and now in Cannes for the day, Mr. Chips, and end your ski adventure on a high note!" Jeff concluded as he held Mr. Chips in his arms and squeezed him until he squealed.

Mr. Chips barked cutely in agreement. What a notable day it was, seeing Mr. Chips water-ski; and what a wonderful, adorable end to a perfectly magical day on the Cote D'Azur!

CHAPTER NINE: MR. CHIPS GOES OUT ON THE TOWN CELEBRATING

After his highly celebrated water-skiing adventure was captured on newsreel for the evening segment on the local Cannes television channel, Mr. Chips could be seen sartorially dressed for his stroll along La Croisette that evening with Jeff and the Vetches in tow. They walked all the way to Da Bouttau, which took quite a while from the Carlton Hotel.

"Let's have the chauffeur pick us up when we're ready to return to the hotel please!" Mrs. Vetch said to Dr. Vetch, "and if the kids want to walk home, they may, if they promise to stay together at that hour of the evening!" Mrs. Vetch insisted, talking directly to her children.

"Yes, mother!" the three of them announced simultaneously as they approached the famed restaurant.

And when they all arrived at the entrance to Da Bouttau, even the eminent Mr. Picasso, who, amazingly was in attendance once again, was impressed with Mr. Chips' artistic flair for clothing, because no schnauzer had ever looked more 'the part', as they say, just like a cool bohemian; for Monsieur Chips was, 'juste parfait' that evening, and the only way to describe the night at Da Bouttau was, 'c'est magnifique!'"

Another gorgeous repast was served by the attentive staff at the famed restaurant, all of whom paid particular attention to pleasing their most special guest, the wonderful and glorious Mr. Chips!

CHAPTER TEN: MR. CHIPS AT THE BERNARD BUFFET EXHIBIT

The very next day, Mrs. Vetch told everyone in the family that she wanted to go see the exhibit of Bernard Buffet's paintings of the French Riviera at one of the local galleries.

"Do we have to go?" Sharon asked, "Alec and I would rather sightsee along the coast and see Etz today," she added, "please take Jeff and Mr. Chips with you because they'd be far better and more interesting companions!" Sharon mentioned.

"I have to agree with her there!" Dr. Vetch stated.

"OK, then, Jeff and Mr. Chips will join us at the art exhibit in town if they wish!" Mrs. Vetch agreed, and it was all settled. Mr. Chips scampered around the room; and Jeff helped him put on a casual lightweight sweater vest, bowler hat, dark shades and flip flops for that debonair look of 'je ne c'est quoi'.

When they arrived at the gallery, Mr. Chips barked his approval of the most impressive canvas, featuring Mr. Buffet's thickly applied brushstrokes of rich color showcasing the outdoor scene of the waterfront of Cannes with the image of the Carlton Hotel situated in the center of the enormous painting.

Like the artist, Mr. Chips had an eye for flair; and if ever a painter embodied it, it was Bernard Buffet, with his bright splashy canvases, thickly applied paint and iconic recognizable scenes that he made look so special through light and shadow, texture and paint applied with a style unmatched in contemporary art.

And Mr. Chips, who gavotted in front of the large canvas, instantly was drawn to the work, as was Jeff, who was determined to own one day one of the beautiful canvases of Mr. Buffet.

When Mrs. Vetch said, "we're buying the large painting of the Carlton Hotel," the very one that Jeff stood in front of and that had captivated the dancing Mr. Chips, it was pure kismet. "Someday it will be yours!" Mrs. Vetch whispered to her young son as she winked at him knowingly. And for Jeff, it didn't get better than that!

CHAPTER ELEVEN: MR. CHIPS FLIES SKY HIGH

The very next day, Mr. Chips got his wish to parasail with Jeff, who'd secured him in a special harness on his back while Jeff skied behind a motorboat that traversed the beachfront near the Carlton Hotel's seaside umbrellas. Once they'd gotten up sufficient steam and the motorboat was going fast enough, Jeff let out his portable parachute; and they were lifted into the air, soaring as high as the top floor of the Carlton Hotel, which shimmered a bright white in the heat of the midday sun.

All the tourists along the quays of the port and the sidewalks of La Croisette stared toward the bay where Jeff and Mr. Chips were parasailing; and they, along with the passengers onboard *Seacloud,* as well as the patrons of Da Bouttau and the guests of the Carlton Hotel, all waved as Jeff and Mr. Chips parasailed on by the entirety of the Cannes waterfront until, at last, Jeff began his descent to the applause of the waterfront crowds, who rushed to the beach in front of the Carlton Hotel, where Jeff let go of the tow rope and skied right up onto the sand with the deflated parachute dragging behind him as the newspaper reporters and their crews photographed and recorded the entire scene for later rebroadcast.

While perhaps not as dramatic as the original plan of putting Mr. Chips on a miniature chair with skis for his feet and that would have been attached to a kite Jeff had tricked out especially for a flyover of Cannes, it was far safer for Jeff to parasail then Mr. Chips, who had a wonderful time, just the same!

It was a truly great way to bring to a close Mr. Chips enjoyable visit to the French Riviera!

CHAPTER TWELVE: MR. CHIPS FLIES HOME FIRST CLASS!

Only first-class air travel would do for a first-class guy like Mr. Chips! After wowing them on the Cote D'Azur, Mr. Chips traveled home to Chicago in style, wined and dined, pampered and puffed the only way the cutest schnauzer in the world could be! The stewardesses on board Air France saw to it that Mr. Chips was given every treat which a cool celebrity pooch deserved; and because he was a unique canine celebrity, both he and his best friend Jeff were handled with extra special care and kid gloves by the best airline cabin crew anywhere.

When they landed at Midway, Mr. Chips was treated like royalty by the Air France attendants, not because of his eminent lineage, but because of his well-known joie de vie, the international fame of his accomplishments and his canine diplomacy in showing the wonderful people of France just

LOUIS W.HIRSCHMANN

how fabulous we Americans from across the pond could be. And, thanks to the fine people of Air France, the end of the trip and return home was as lovely as the rest of it had been!

****

When last Mr. Chips was seen in the backyard of the Vetch family home in Glencoe, the cutest puppy in the world was scampering around the backyard, digging up the tan bark underneath where Jeff was on his swing set, then running over and barking at the imperiously arrogant red roses, who were saucily gavotting in the summer breeze.

Oodles, the neighbor's cat was chasing Hazelnut and her buddy, Johnnie, the friendly neighborhood squirrel, right on up into the Vetch's maple tree; and Mr. Chips barked at all of them to come down that very instant and help him dig a small trench in the ravine down by the slope of the backyard.

You see, Mr. Chips had no time to think further about his trip to the French Riviera because he needed to free the dam of water being held back by a bunch of fallen leaves that were in danger of flooding the bluebells that clung to their precarious purchase by the side of the meandering rivulet. Otherwise, it would eventually break through the leaf pile and cause a flood all the way from the backyard neighbors' bramble obscured storm pipe downslope to the sewer drain near Dundee Road, a relatively short distance that appeared much larger to a puppy and his caretaker.

Oodles, Hazelnut and Johnnie ignored all the wailing and plaintive barking of Mr. Chips, who stopped, smelled the bluebells, looked up and felt the sun on his back while remembering when he was waterskiing on the Cote D'Azur.

****

Was the Cote D'Azur just a dream of Mr. Chips? Could any of this charming tale of Mr. Chips' adventures on the French Riviera have really happened to just an ordinary schnauzer running around his backyard in a small midwestern town?

Only Mr. Chips knew the truth. And that day, he was wearing a navy beret he won, and a gift of a shining necklace designed in script that said 'XOXOS from Picasso', proof enough of the veracity of this tale without his verbally revealing a thing.

Then, of course, there was that day, not so very long ago, when, just as he looked skyward from the backyard at a butterfly flutter by, Mr. Chips heard Dr. Vetch through the opened sliding glass doors of the sunroom call out to Mrs. Vetch,

"Doe, there's a small letter the size of a thank you note from the Windsors addressed to Mr. Chips and care of Jeff. Should we open it?"

"No dear, please save it for Master Jeffrey and Mr. Chips please, thanks, dear!"

And there you have it! There's no more to be said, other than, 'merci beaucoup to Jeff, au revoir and goodbye, Mr. Chips!'

THE END

BOOKS BY THIS AUTHOR

Parallax Reflections

A compelling coming-of-age story of a harrowing weekend in the life of Jeff Vetch, a teenage heir and budding represented author, who battles his inner demons as well as bullies at his posh New England prep school.

Jeff gears up for the fight of his life against his Chicago high-society family who resent his scandalous tell-all diary being published. But perceptions can be different, as Jeff's siblings tell their own stories of what happened that fateful weekend.

Those "parallax reflections" make up a wonderfully entertaining fictional novel by Louis W. Hirschmann, who has written several novels inspired by his life growing up in the Midwest.

Fireflies Of Summer

In this exciting companion novel to "Parallax Reflections", narrator Jeff Vetch takes a train up to a Wisconsin summer camp in 1963, where he prepares for the adventure of a lifetime at the age of thirteen. A sudden tragedy unfolds, and young Vetch must come to terms with the unexplained death of his camp counselor in the only way he knows how... by discovering the truth. A sweet, beautifully written and poignant novel by author Louis W. Hirschmann.

The Old Surprise Shop

In this charming prequel to the novels "Fireflies of Summer" and "Parallax Reflections", the adult narrator Jeff Vetch dreams on Christmas Eve of his early teenage years in his beloved hometown, where he remembers the Christmas tree in the toy shop window. Each of the ornaments reflects a scene he relives from his childhood. When he awakens from his dream, Jeff has a new appreciation for his life, his memories and his future. He is a changed man, a better man, for it.

The Lost Island Of Mystery Lake

In this sequel to "Fireflies of Summer", the narrator Jeff Vetch and his boyhood friend Zeke spend a summer trying to save Zeke's family's ancestral lands on Lost Island from greedy developers who want to destroy its natural beauty and turn it into another tacky resort, against the wishes of Zeke's dying father. Weaving a multi-generational one-hundred-year saga, the author explores the meaning of friendship, family and their fight for sacred lands held in trust.

Shadows Upon The Seine

In this charming jewel box of a tale, an American boy visiting Paris comes of age in the early 1960's when he learns the meaning of love and remembrance, of friendship and desire-- all intermingled in a light-hearted story with a surprising twist at the end! By the author of "Fireflies of Summer" and "The Lost Island of Mystery Lake".

Returning To Melrose

While on holiday on the west coast with his family, young Jeff Vetch visits a famous studio and meets well-known celebrities in an amazing autograph hunt! He meets new friends who help him understand the meaning of family, friendship and generosity in this heartwarming coming of age tale set in Los Angeles during the early 1960s.

Author Louis W. Hirschmann has written numerous novels featuring beloved character Jeffrey Vetch, as he grows from youth to manhood in the mid-20th Century.

East Of Eagle

Reporters from the local newspaper visit Jeff Vetch at his La Jolla residence to chat with him about his lifetime of creative writing and his many published works.

The discussion quickly centers on a subject the reporters are most interested in-- a tragic weekend fifty years earlier at the Vetch family summer home which Jeff had written about in one of his books.

What really happened in Eagle River that summer of 1969? A twist of fate reveals the ultimate truth in the always-dramatic, very fictional world of the Vetch Family, a series of novels written by Louis W. Hirschmann.

Mezzanine At The Breakers

Sparks fly the moment teenager Jeff Vetch meets young tennis pro Tony at one of the most glamorous tennis courts in the world, at the famed Breakers Hotel of Palm Beach!

During one unforgettable winter vacation, Jeff discovers more about Tony and himself than he ever could have imagined when he mistakenly exits the elevator on the mezzanine level of the iconic hotel and steps into a sexy adventure. A smartly written, poignant and provocative gay coming-of-age story, written by Louis W.

Hirschmann.

From Round Hill With Love

In this novel about a young man's vacation at a famous Jamaica resort, the narrator Jeff Vetch, reflects on the unforgettable time he shared there with friends and family. From deep sea dangers he experiences to a lost treasure hunt for a priceless gem, this tale is replete with famous people whom Jeff meets along the way on the island. His vacation is one he'll remember forever and so will the reader! Another charming novel featuring the adventures of character Jeff Vetch, written by Louis W. Hirschmann.

Made in the USA
Columbia, SC
15 June 2024